LOCKDOWN HORROR #4

I0593130

Compiled & Edited by
Ben Thomas | D. Kershaw | S.N. Graves

Cover design	Dawn Burdett	www.dmburdett.com
Formatting	Ben Thomas	www.blackharepress.com
Editing	D. Kershaw	www.blackharepress.com
	S.N. Grave	swww.sngraves.com
Read Team	David Green	davidgreenwritercom.wordpress.com
	Jennifer Hatfield	jhatfieldauthor.wixsite.com/website
	Jodi Jensen	jodijensenwrites.wordpress.com
	Lyndsay Ellis-Holloway	authorlyndseyellisholloway.webador.co.uk
	Maggie Pawsey	
	Stacey Jaine McIntosh	www.staceyjainemcintosh.com

TABLE OF
CONTENTS

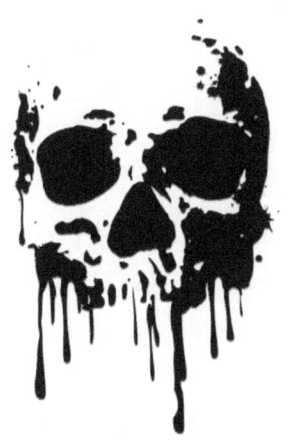

SILENCE FINDS ME

By J.W. Garrett

I wake to silence, bloodied hands. The room in disarray. Nothing as it should be. Stumbling to a stand, something draws me ahead. My eyes narrow to a world that doesn't make sense. Dead. All of them.

9

Looks like a giant animal got loose. My body trembles. I throw open a window.

More *horror*.

More half eaten corpses.

I drag in a breath, needing courage for the scene behind me. My body seizes, wrenching in pain. A noise sounds that isn't human. I writhe, fighting; the transformation takes over. Glancing in the reflection of the window, the horror is me.

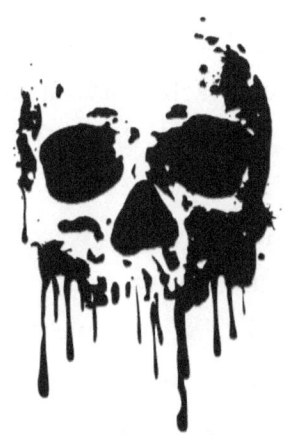

HOUSE ARREST

By Beth W. Patterson

I don't want to have to do this. Some people taste blood in their mouths when they feel fear, and this is certainly the case for me.

You seem to enjoy this power trip. My

invited guest, you almost immediately began the scare tactics; how dangerous it is for a young woman to live by herself in such a big house.

Your hypothetical warning reveals your true monstrosity. "By the time that window breaks," you tell me, "it's too late. I've already got you."

No, you don't. I throw aside the wooden stake and make a lunge for your neck.

HOFFMAN'S CREEPER

By Cameron Trost

Professor Samuel Hoffman spent most of his waking hours in his extensive greenhouse, where he attended to his collection of rare plants with obsessive fervour. The botanist's long and celebrated career had been dedicated to the discovery and study of the world's remaining unknown varieties of herbaceous life-forms. And his retirement was being spent in exactly the same manner. His professional life had been one of astounding success. From the venerable halls of Oxford to the modern campus of Berkeley, he had taught a new generation of scientific minds about the exotic species that he had discovered and named.

His work had also taken him far from the lecture theatres and laboratories of the world's finest universities. Over the years, Hoffman's expeditions had seen him slash his way through the gorilla and guerrilla occupied jungles of Africa, and trudge across the endless glacial plains of Siberia, always with the same objective in mind: the discovery of the unknown. Hundreds of new species of plants had been brought to light thanks to his tireless dedication, and dozens of botanical volumes proudly bore his name. His life's work assured his place as one of the greatest botanists since the golden age of exploration when the likes of Carl Linnaeus and Sir Joseph Banks had sailed across uncharted waters and documented virgin lands and the mysterious treasures they hosted.

***

Professor Hoffman finished his cup of breakfast tea before heading towards the greenhouse. The glass structure was almost as big as the rest of the house, a Victorian manor that had always been his home.

He had married at the age of twenty-four but never had children. His insatiable passion for plants had quickly suffocated his wife's passion for him. Their marriage hadn't lasted long and had left Professor Hoffman with nothing more than a few old photographs, a bitter taste in his mouth, and an even stronger desire to dedicate himself entirely to his work.

The absence of a family might have caused an observer who didn't understand the man to think that he was lonely. However, if such a person were ever to suggest this impression to Professor Hoffman, he would have been met not with an expression of sadness or contempt but rather a portrait of pure bewilderment. The professor had never considered himself lonely. Indeed, he had all the company he needed within the confines of his greenhouse. From time to time, he had contact with other humans, although it was generally limited to a close circle of former colleagues, students, and members of the botanical community.

"Good morning," he greeted his plants. Even a great scientific mind like his had some room for one or two illogical habits. Professor Hoffman did have children after all. They just weren't of the warm-blooded kind.

The greenhouse was separated into two sections. Just as sons and daughters would need their own bedrooms, different plants required different environments.

He checked the temperature and humidity of both sections by looking at the thermometer and hygrometer placed in the middle of each. Then, assured that everything was in order, he began inspecting his specimens, one by one. The professor noted any changes in condition, whether negative or positive. His records were meticulous and detailed, nothing went unnoticed.

His dionaea muscipulae, known to the uninitiated as Venus Flytraps, were waiting with their mouths wide open like hungry nestlings begging for their mother to feed them worms. But his notebook reminded him that it was too early to feed them. Too much nutrition could be just as detrimental as too little. They would have to be patient.

The fluorescent pseudomonads were in good condition, just as they had been during the night. He often inspected them when it was dark so that he could appreciate their subtle glow.

Only very rare plants deserved to occupy a place in Professor Hoffman's greenhouse. There was no room for everyday, run-of-the-mill garden varieties. At least one specimen of most of the species he had discovered could be found in his care. But, unfortunately, he had lost some of his discoveries; even his expert and thorough attention hadn't been enough to preserve them. Worse still, he had been unable to save some species of which his specimen had been the only one. Once, after the loss of his deppea splendens, he had fallen into a deep depression and only succeeded in drawing himself out of it because an acquaintance had made him understand that he owed it to his other specimens.

Professor Hoffman continued his inspection, jotting down notes as he did so. He used a magnifying glass to study each plant in detail.

His collection of the nepenthes genus, or monkey cups, was worthy of the greatest accolades. The sarracenia and utricularia genera were also featured in strength and his collection was quite possibly the best in the world outside of their natural climates.

Professor Hoffman watered those plants that required it. Certain plants required certain nutrients. Others needed particular water dispensing instruments, from pencil thin pipettes and spray bottles to watering cans of various sizes. He knew which plants required which kind of treatment and his notebook allowed him to keep track of the frequency.

The botanist was able to concentrate on his work without any disturbance. Visitors were seldom and when an acquaintance did come, it was never before morning tea.

He was hidden from view by the leafy trees that bordered his large property and little noise reached his failing ears. He listened to music as he worked. Some botanists claimed that gentle music helped plants grow. But, despite several attempts at verifying this hypothesis, Professor

Hoffman couldn't find any basis to the claim. He simply listened to the music for his own pleasure. Once upon a time, there had been several dogs in the area and their barking had penetrated the panes of the glasshouse while he worked, but now there were none, they had all disappeared and hadn't been replaced.

Soft sunlight entered through the glass roof of the greenhouse and touched the botanist's pale, balding head as he worked. He was in paradise, surrounded by plant-life, the only kind of life that meant anything to him. People were to him as shrubs were to other people and animals were like blades of grass or patches of moss: sometimes useful but nothing very special.

The professor whistled to the calm music of Bach as he moved from a row of exquisite Thai Euphorbia flowers to a rectangular pot that hosted recently germinated oroxylum indicum, commonly known as Midnight Horror. He smiled to himself as he admired the impeccable condition and steady growth of these extremely rare tropical plants. He examined them with his magnifying glass and stopped whistling just long enough to sound a hum of satisfaction.

"Excellent," he said as he carefully noted his observations.

All was as it should have been in the Hoffman greenhouse, all except for one hungry plant, a member of the family whose demands the patriarch had trouble meeting. However much the professor gave, it was never enough to sate this plant's appetite.

A dark cloud covered his face as he laid his eyes upon it. He didn't know how much longer it would survive, and the prospect of losing it made him feel sick inside.

The creeper covered most of the southern end of the greenhouse. It grew very slowly, but over the fifteen years that it had been in his care, it had continued to spread out lethargically. At present, it covered an area of about three square metres. The creeper's five-fingered claws held onto the perfectly smooth pane of the southern wall. That in itself was astounding. More remarkable yet, the botanist had once tried to pry one of the claws free just to see if he could, but that seemingly simple task had proven impossible. The claw had been as stubborn as the donkey the professor had once bought for far too many pesos from an unscrupulous old man in Mexico.

The plant's determination to resist any attempt to detach it from where it grew was not its only astonishing feature. Its beauty was what had most struck Professor Hoffman the day he first encountered it. To say that the creeper was a thing of beauty would be like calling an oak a strong tree. It was without doubt the most formidably stunning life-form on the planet. As far as the botanist was concerned, it was far more stunning and elegant than any human female ever to have graced the Earth.

The creeper's small round leaves shone brightly despite the gentle sunlight, and the impossibly delicate red flowers that adorned its maze of tubes were more exquisite than any orchid or rose he had ever seen.

Professor Hoffman could still clearly remember the day he discovered the creeping vine. It was so rare that only a handful of people outside of the micro-climate where it grew had ever even heard of it, and as far as he knew, there were only two such specimens kept in captivity anywhere in the world. The professor had not yet visited the other site, but he had a photograph of it, and it was clear that the other specimen was much better nurtured than his. He had written an entire book about the exotic creeper, but in it, he only told part of the story. He wanted to keep some of the details of his discovery to himself, as selfish as that may have seemed.

***

Fifteen years earlier and on the other side of the world, Professor Hoffman had been exploring one of the remotest parts of the planet—the rainforests of the Cape York Peninsula in Australia. It was at a time during his career when he had benefited from an abundance of research grants and a burning desire to discover plants that were still unknown to the scientific community. He had journeyed into the territory of the Ayapathu aborigines accompanied by several post-graduate students from Cooktown. What he remembered most about the densely forested region was the humidity and the mosquitoes. The two went hand in hand, making the trek through the virgin rainforest all the more painful.

The Ayapathu people hadn't spoken much English and all of the communication between Hoffman and the aborigines had been through a young interpreter from Cooktown. The botanist had asked them questions about unusual plants in the forest and listened to their replies. He had taken no interest in them beyond the call of duty. Human customs and such anthropological matters were of no concern to him at all. He had been aware that many people disliked the native population through bigotry and racism, some didn't even think of them as human beings, but for the obsessed botanist, the reason behind his indifference was the complete opposite, his lack of interest in them was because they *were* human. His mind was one-tracked, it revolved around plants. Its every thought was devoted to all things leafy, greenish, creeping, and sprouting. Human beings, regardless of their ethnicity or culture were just part of the scenery for him, the way he imagined plants must be to other people.

An elderly Ayapathu woman with a round face and long white hair had spoken to the botanist in her strange language. He had become excited as the words spoken by the interpreter reached his ears. She had told him about the amazing creeper and its unbelievable characteristics. The professor, despite having believed only half of what she said, had decided to search for the fabled creeper.

In fact, he hadn't had to search a great deal at all because the woman knew precisely where to find the plant. As it turned out, she looked after it.

If the professor had been a man of ethics, he would have felt guilty about having betrayed the Ayapathu people's trust, but his disinterest in mankind rendered him immune to such bothersome feelings. During the night, he had returned to take the plant, to steal it from its native habitat. It had been growing on the black stump of a fallen tree, and due to the firm grip of the creeper's claws, he had been obliged to take the entire stump with him. That hadn't been a problem. With such an exceptional discovery, nothing was too big an obstacle to overcome.

Professor Hoffman had immediately left the Ayapathu territory with the stolen creeper and within a week had managed to wade through enough paperwork to allow him to leave the country with his botanical jewel. If he had felt the need to do so, he could have tried to imagine how the elderly woman must have reacted upon discovering that the dishonest foreigner had disappeared during the night and taken the plant with him. Of course, the professor hadn't even given her a second thought. She had been no more than a means to an end.

***

Kamu Yuku, that is what she had called it. According to the interpreter, that meant Blood Tree, an apt description if ever there was one. The creeper's tiny red flowers looked like droplets of fresh blood, somehow simultaneously dark and bright. As far as Hoffman was concerned, the Kamu Yuku was a living work of art struggling to survive the trials and tribulations of evolution and climate change. It wasn't an example of survival of the fittest but rather an exception to Darwin's rule. That it had avoided the long list of extinct species for so long was practically a miracle. Hoffman's creeper was an example of survival of the exquisite despite the heavy odds increasingly weighing against it. It was delicate perfection fighting to exist in a world of powerful, hungry weeds.

Helen of Troy, Xi Shi, Cleopatra, these beauties whose lives and loves have long been held dear in the pages of time and the hearts of men throughout the ages were nothing more than hairy mammals to the botanist. The creeper was the real incarnation of beauty—he understood that, even if others didn't, even if posters featuring it would never be stuck on schoolboys' bedroom walls or used to decorate the back of cheap playing cards.

Professor Hoffman rarely thought about women at all, and he almost never thought about his wife who had left him so many years earlier. He didn't wonder where she was or with whom she was living. He didn't even dream about her, not even once in a very long while. In his greenhouse lived all the family he could ever want or need, and he knew that so long as he continued to protect them, they would never betray or abandon him.

He squeezed the trigger of one of his spray bottles, the one that provided the finest spray. Hoffman continued tending to his array of plants, but while he did so, he kept glancing over towards his favourite child. He hoped that its condition would not deteriorate, that the firm grasp of its tiny green claws would continue to hold tight. It needed a great deal of attention. It drank the botanist's time and energy, but that made perfect sense to him. Most things of beauty are very difficult to please, so it was only logical that the most beautiful of beings should be the most exigent.

An unexpected sound interrupted Hoffman's work and thoughts. It was the ring of his deep-toned brass doorbell. It took him so completely by surprise that he almost dropped his spray bottle, an action that would have been disastrous considering that he was holding it over one of his most delicately structured specimens.

"Who could that be?" he muttered to himself. Nobody was due to visit him that day, and his visitors seldom came unannounced.

The professor carefully placed his

spray bottle on the shelf where it belonged, between one slightly larger than it and another ever so slightly smaller. He then made his way towards the front door, making sure to close the door to his greenhouse behind him.

"Hello, mister."

"Hello?" he greeted the little girl with a question.

"Can you help me, please? I hope you can." Her smile stretched out between chestnut pigtails.

He observed her indifferently, wondering why she had disturbed him from his work. Although he didn't recognise her, he guessed that she lived somewhere in the neighbourhood.

"It's my dog, he's disappeared and I

can't find him anywhere."

"A lot of dogs have disappeared around here," Hoffman informed her.

"I know." Despite her smile, he could see that she was feeling sad.

"When did it disappear?"

"Not it, *he*," she corrected him. "About a week ago."

"What happened to your hand?"

She looked at her hand. It was scratched and bleeding a little.

"It's nothing. I just fell over in the street. It's all right. So have you seen him?"

Hoffman seemed distracted and not in the slightest sympathetic.

"Seen whom?"

"My dog." She looked at him strangely but kept smiling politely.

"Oh, yes, of course. I think I have, in fact. There's a dog in my garden. I don't know where it came from. Maybe it's yours."

She pushed her way inside and ran through the house.

"Wait!" Hoffman called after her. "Be careful! Don't run!" He wasn't concerned about her but rather about what would happen if the child got into the greenhouse. He thought about the expression 'a bull in a china shop'.

His aging limbs couldn't move him fast enough to catch her, and before he could do anything about it, the little girl had made her way into the greenhouse in search of her lost dog.

"Where is he?"

Hoffman arrived in the greenhouse, gasping for breath and looking pale with fear. The child was standing just centimetres away from his beloved creeper and staring at it, all thought of her wayward dog instantly forgotten.

"It's... Wow!" she said.

"It certainly is," he agreed, catching his breath. "But it's not in good shape unfortunately."

He picked up a watering pot and a pruning implement and approached the little visitor from behind.

"I need to take better care of it. You can help me."

***

That evening, once his daily work had been completed and he had cleaned up,

Professor Hoffman sat back in his armchair with his most prized photograph album. He opened it and stared at one of the images on the first page. The creeper shown covered most of the south side of a spacious country manor. The unusually shaped greenhouse that protected it had obviously been tailor-made. The size of that creeper put Professor Hoffman's to shame. No matter how hard he tried to sate his own creeper's appetite, it would never rival the specimen of Kamu Yuku shown in the photo.

The botanist closed the album and sighed. If only his creeper could grow and flourish with such vivacity. But he knew that he couldn't safely compete with that kind of audacity. He wondered how many dogs, cats, and little children had been reported missing in the area around the manor in the photograph.

First published in *Hoffman's Creeper and Other Disturbing Tales*, Black Beacon Books, 2013

BLACK HARE PRESS

A MAN WALKED INTO A BAR AND SAID...

By Diane Arrelle

Henry held the gun in his right hand, weighing the decision whether to kill himself or not. The frigid air plumed around his face as he breathed. "Damn I'm tired of it all. Cold, tired and…"

"Henwy Baby, whatcha doing?"

He looked away from the weapon as a shiver started at the base of his spine and worked its way upward. That god awful chalk-on-blackboard voice chilled him, chilled him more than the ever-constant cold that gnawed at him day after day, year after year, decade after decade and, fearfully he realised, century after century ever could.

"Trying to get warm," he muttered, knowing the only way to be warm in this existence was to fuck that bitch, fuck her as she clawed his flesh to ribbons with her steel nails while she cried out constantly in that voice.

"Well, Henwy Wenwy," she lisped and threw her head back to make her mane of platinum blond curls sway enticingly. "I can warm wou wup."

He thought about the scabs on his back. "Later, I need time to heal."

She pursed her perfect red lips into a well-practiced pout and shrugged her naked shoulders, causing round size D breasts to bounce ever so slightly. "OK, just wemember, you're the one who's cold."

Henry snorted. How could he forget? Since the moment he walked into that bar all those years ago, the only thing he had forgotten was what comfort was.

All he did that fateful day was down a couple of beers and say, "Shit, I'd sell my soul to never see the human race again. Hell, just give me one beautiful woman to spend forever with and I'd be a happy man."

He shoulda known a bar named Beelzebub's was a front.

A few drinks later, with some encouragement from the bartender, he'd told the guy what he wanted from life—that special woman who was hot enough to warm his bones and no one else to ever bother him again.

The next thing he knew he was signing a contract with his blood, so he added the 'I want to live forever clause', to make sure he beat the devil.

Now, because of one bad day at work, a speeding ticket, and a few drinks, here he sat, reading his copy of the thousand-page contract for the thousandth time. The only way out of this frozen version of Hell was suicide, and that meant an eternity of burning in the other version of Hell. He was doomed to live like this, in his own special eternity, a bleak place of bitter cold, no other living soul except for the demon bitch and absolutely nothing else. He'd forgotten to add comfort and distractions like books and music and art to his list of needs. He'd forgotten about food, drink, love and clothes.

He was freezing and bored and although he could be hurt and feel pain, he could not die, except by his own hand. He couldn't even get the satisfaction of killing her. He tried choking that voice into silence once. He'd wrung her neck until she bled, but then she'd sat right back up and laughed at him.

"Oh Henwy, was that as good for you as it was for me?" she had croaked out, her voice even more abrasive to his ears.

He shivered at the memory and stared at his life-mate with her talon nails, her exquisitely perfect body that had absolutely no appeal left, and he knew red-hot hatred. For a brief second that hate actually pushed away the ever-present chill.

"Why are you here with me?" he asked, trying to fuel the fire of loathing.

"Because I wove you, Henwy," she screeched.

"No, you don't," he sighed as the gnawing cold returned to his bones. "Why are you here?"

She gave no answer.

"We've been together so long, yet you never talk to me, only at me. All you want is sex. Why did you end up here in this frozen wasteland with me? What bargain did you strike?"

She stood there looking at her nails.

He pointed the gun at her. "Answer me, damn it!"

She laughed.

He cocked the trigger. "Even if you can't die, this'll hurt, you know."

She laughed harder and spoke in a clear, rich voice. "Oh Henry, I can't die. I can't hurt. I didn't strike a deal. Eternity means nothing. Eventually you will kill yourself and my job will be done. Then I can go home, back to Him. Back where I belong."

"You really are a Demon!" he said and pulled the trigger.

She staggered back, laughing again. The hole in her gut closed. "Henwy, you silly wabbit," she said, lisping back into persona. "Wanna scwew, Henwy Wenwy?"

Henry looked around this room, his entire world, and turned away. Although he knew the text by heart, he began to read the contract again. That would fill some time. When he healed from their last round, he'd have sex, just to be warm for a minute or two.

He put the gun in a drawer for safekeeping. He knew why it was the only thing in that room besides the contract, desk, chair and bed. Because, someday, he would be able to welcome death. Someday the warmth of an eternal Hell would be worth it.

First published in *Just A Drop In The Cup*, **Darker Intentions Press, 2007**

THE LAST TANGO

By E.L. Giles

A great melancholy surged into Garcia as he gazed at the vacant seat in front of him. The bottle of tequila lay overturned on the table, empty. The last drop had been siphoned, but the grief hadn't left.

Something of a masochistic habit persisted, though, and Garcia's eyes traced the path from the kitchen down to the living room and stopped. Everything in the house reminded him about his solitude, and the reigning silence deafeningly screamed out in the midst of her absence. Garcia let a long sigh escape him. He would have given anything for one last tango with her.

As he often did when the weight of his loss became too heavy, Garcia switched on the turntable. The bewitching chords of guitars quickly filled the house while he sat down in the dim salon. Garcia felt drained. His mind searched for ghosts that didn't exist. He longed to feel her again. The way her hair brushed against his cheeks. The soft contact of her lips upon his. The sensation of their bodies interlaced in a transcendent dance.

"You miss her, do you?" The voice came from Garcia's side. Turning his head, all he could see were the impressions left on the faded sofa where she used to sit. Empty. The voice repeated, "You miss her, do you?"

Garcia, too tired to twitch or jump at hearing the spectral voice, answered simply, "I do."

"What would you do to be able to dance with her one last time?" the voice asked, soothing, friendly, but with something in it that should have filled Garcia with dread.

Intrigued, Garcia said, his voice breaking, "I would give my life away."

The guitar music travelled the room in mystical interludes, soft and languid. Every slide of the fingers over the strings sent electrical waves up Garcia's spine. Every chord invited him to leave his current lethargy. His feet burned with excitation. His hands prickled with desire.

"Yes, I would give my life away for one last tango with her."

When Garcia turned his head again, alerted by the frantic rhythm of feet tapping on the hard floor, a pirouetting shape welcomed his shocked eyes. Suddenly, the room burst into colour and was filled with liveliness. Garcia's spirit lifted, attracted by the echoes of her breathing and the rustling of her skirt against her moving legs. And while the melody of the guitars rose into a rousing crescendo, Garcia jumped off his chair.

He strode across the room, his legs possessed by the devil of tango, and as the rhythm dropped to a restful series of notes, she stretched her hand out. Garcia took it, focusing on the warmth that crawled up his arm. Slowly, the song accelerated. The two bodies joined together and followed music and movements long forgotten. His skin blazed longingly. His heart galloped unstoppably. Her hair whipped his face gently as she spun, leaving in its wake the soft smell of lavender. Garcia inhaled deeply. His eyes couldn't leave her iridescent irises. His hand couldn't leave the curve of her waist. Their bodies twirled and swirled, fully consumed by the wild climax of their impossible dance.

And when the last twangs of the guitars and the echoes of their strings died out, the moment passed. Too quickly, Garcia's colourful world dulled to the sombre grey of his heart. One last touch of her dark skin, during which the warmth evaporated with her shadow, and she was gone. A hand, invisible yet unmistakably there, landed on Garcia's shoulder, making him turn around.

"You gave me your life," the voice said, pointing at Garcia's inert body seated on the chair in the corner of the room, "and I gave you one last tango with her."

BRING HIM BACK

By Evan Baughfman

Hell found me.

Hell found me. He'll find me.

The woman did her best to ignore the stupid autocorrect on her phone and in her journal began to copy down her list of deepest desires, which she had generated during her lunch break the day before. Writing down this wish list by her own hand was one step of many that would hopefully bring her husband back to her.

Earlier, the woman had filled a pen with her own blood. Now, she began to carefully transcribe an ancient chant from a weathered copy of Julio Smith's critically acclaimed book, *Shortcuts for the Sorcerer in You*.

Two weeks ago, her husband had left their weekend cabin and gone for a hike in the woods. A bloody scrap of his yellow tank top was all that was found of him. *Sorry, ma'am, but he was most likely eaten by a bear*, the experts had told her.

The woman wished to hug her husband

hard, hug him long. At least one last time.

Even if he was, indeed, dead. In fact, she expected him to be dead.

The only other explanation was far too difficult for her to believe: that he had run away from her. What she was about to do could only work if his love for her was pure and true.

Awash in moonlight, she kissed her wedding ring six times, just as the book instructed. She read aloud the words she wrote slowly, and as clearly, as she could.

When she was done, she watched the edge of the woods from the bedroom window.

But a minute passed. Two. Three. Nothing happened.

The woman slipped into her favourite

dress and studied herself in the mirror, realising that she needed a little makeup to cover the bags under her eyes. But it also got her thinking…

How would her husband look when he eventually came? She imagined a rotting thing full of maggots, staggering to her, parts falling off or missing, eaten by scavenging creatures...

She went into the living room, switched on the lamp, sat on the couch, and waited.

One hour passed. Two. Three.

Her heart raced. She had heard bloody, tragic stories about what happened when tainted love was forced to live again.

Knock, knock, knock.

She wiped sweaty palms on the back

of her dress and practically ran to the front door. She threw it open, ready to take her husband in again, no matter his current state.

She gasped. There was no one there.

Something tugged at the bottom of her dress. She looked down, and there at her feet was a severed arm, a piece of jagged bone sticking out at its shoulder. Its hand waved to her.

It was her husband's left arm. She recognized the scar on the elbow from when he had slipped in the bathtub as a boy. And there was his matching wedding band on the ring finger. The back of the hand was scratched deeply, and the pinky finger now ended in a bloody stump.

"What the *hell*?" She hoped the dark

gods were listening. "All that work for an *arm*?"

The woman bent over and grabbed the arm by the wrist. It shook a "peace" sign at her with its index and middle fingers.

"I'm not going to hurt you. Let's go see if we can make this work."

She carried the arm back into the cabin and closed the front door. "Sorry if it's a little chilly in here."

She placed the appendage gently onto the couch and went into the bedroom. She threw open the book of incantations and scanned the page from which she lifted the chant.

In small type, next to an asterisk, it read, *Upon completion of this spell, the wedding bands will be reunited. For it is the promise of taking one's hand in marriage that is most precious. Therefore, anything more than the reunion of the bands is not guaranteed.*

The woman sighed. She opened the closet, rummaged through a box, pulled out her husband's yellow mittens and a red Christmas stocking.

Back in the living room, the woman said, "I brought mittens. I guess you only need one. And if you get into this stocking, you'll probably be extra-toasty."

The arm wriggled in approval and crawled into her lap, lifting its hand for her. The wedding band on its bloated ring finger glowed in the lamplight.

She quickly slipped a mitten onto the hand and pulled the stocking over the arm's stump.

The arm climbed from her lap and made a sharp left off the couch. It lay sprawled on the floor. It flipped itself over and slithered forward. Into a leg of the coffee table.

Apparently, the mitten had rendered the arm blind.

The woman removed the mitten. She laughed. The arm raised its middle finger.

"Now, there's no need to be crude."

It began to pet the top of her right foot, massaging her just below the arch.

"Oh, wow." Just like her husband used to do it.

Then she felt a pinch, and, with a reflexive kick from her other foot, she sent the arm tumbling. It lay still for a moment, dazed. It stretched its fingers and came back to her feet.

"No pinching this time."

The arm made a circle with its thumb and index finger. *Perfect. No problem.*

It grabbed her foot again and worked its magic. "God, that's *great*."

Another pinch. Harder this time. Sharper.

She kicked the arm away again. It was no reflexive action. The stocking fell off the arm.

The woman glared. "If you can't give a decent foot massage, what good *are* you?"

No reply. Not even a middle finger.

"Do I need to get a box and bury you deeper into the forest than you've ever been?"

The arm shot up the couch and leapt for her. Its hand clamped down upon her mouth. The woman stumbled and dug into the arm with her nails as it tried to wrap around her throat.

She lifted it from her face and threw it across the room, knocking the lamp onto its side. Light splashed across one corner of the room and stayed there.

The woman stood in the darkness, gasping for breath. She had to kill the arm somehow.

But the damned limb was fast, and it was on her again, this time stopping at her waist. It began to squeeze. She couldn't believe how strong it was. It was a thing possessed.

She heard, and definitely felt, a couple ribs on her left side break as the arm constricted her like a python. She felt the hand at her spine steadying itself, and then she *knew*.

She had got what she wished for: one last hug from her husband, one last good-bye.

Her eyes bulged as she watched her shadow struggle against the wall. The arm squeezed harder, she let out a banshee wail, and the front door slammed open, nearly breaking off its hinges.

A brown bear sauntered into the cabin.

The arm suddenly released its hold and fell to the floor. It scrambled away somewhere.

The woman staggered over to the couch,

holding her side, trying to catch her breath. Her

heart hammered against broken ribs.

To the bear, she said, "I know you're still inside that thing, Bill. I summoned every part of you here."

The animal was silent. Its head was held low in her direction.

"But you have to go. I can't deal with you like this!"

Something was off about the bear. Its pelt was mangy. Patchy. The woman caught glimpses of the creature's sun-bleached bone in the moonlight. Unhealthy portions of the beast's left side were missing, ripped away, as if they had been lost in a gory battle with a larger predator. Or a big rig truck.

How the hell could the bear still be moving around with wounds like that?

The flesh on its skull was also peeling like weathered wallpaper. Its right eye was an oozing, open sore. Even worse, the animal smelled like rotten meat. Not because that's what its diet consisted of, but because the beast *was* rotten meat.

The dismembered arm was not the only undead thing creeping around in the woods.

The zombear growled, and a piece of its snout fell away from its face, splattering against the floor.

The monster charged.

The woman screamed. The zombear crashed through the coffee table, slamming into the couch, flipping the piece of furniture onto its back. The animal tumbled along with the couch and thundered into the lamplight in front of the woman.

She shrieked, and the zombear roared. It had the arm pinned beneath one of its paws. The appendage wriggled in terror. It waved a futile peace sign at the beast. The zombear drooled.

The woman held a hand over her mouth to stifle her cries. A bloody piece of her husband's yellow tank top was stuck between the zombear's jagged teeth.

The beast's jaws descended over the struggling arm. Bone cracked. The arm lay still.

The zombear fed. Because of its size, the arm had to be torn apart into smaller pieces.

"*Bill!*"

The zombear turned to her. Its lone eye was a dead black pool. No, her husband wasn't in there.

The animal had merely come to finish the meal it had started. Bill must have been tasty. His kisses had always been so sweet.

The zombear turned from the woman, snorted. It picked up what was left of the arm in its jaws, walked around the couch, and strolled back out through the front door into the night.

The woman sat in silence for a few moments. She finally let out a long sigh of relief. She was about to stand when she noticed something lying on the floor in front of her.

A ring finger, dead, bitten off.

And, attached to it, a wedding band, gleaming in the lamplight.

The woman knelt down to retrieve the finger. She removed her husband's ring. She wondered how much it might earn her at the pawnshop back in town.

Floorboards creaked.

The undead bear had returned. Of course, a single scrumptious arm hadn't been enough to quell the creature's relentless hunger pangs.

This time, the zombear didn't watch the woman from the front doorway. It came straight for her, food the only thought on its starving mind.

The woman tossed her husband's finger at the animal, hoping she could distract it like some dog focused on a yummy treat. But the woman's aim wasn't true. The finger bounced off the top of the zombear's head, bending back one of its moldy, maggoty ears.

The monster was upon the woman less than a second later. It swatted her down with a powerful blow and then held her to the floor.

It filled its jaws with her shrieking face.

First published in *Undead 2017*, *The Sirens Call*'s, December 2017

IN MUCK AND MIRE

By Galina Trefil

As she pulled the car to the side of the road, Nell Allred took a long, deep breath. And then another and another. She squeezed her eyes shut, feeling dizziness taking over as those breaths somehow seemed to fail to make it into her lungs. Oh no. Not another panic attack! That was the last thing that Jeremy needed to see! She grabbed a paper bag out of the glove box, held it up to her face, and began to hyperventilate. Gradually, her head slumped against the window as the tried-and-true method began to work its healing magic. When she regained herself, she looked into the back seat. The six-year-old boy there stared away from her, out at the moors that they'd parked beside, seemingly oblivious to his mother's distress.

"How's it going, pal? You good?" she inquired softly, knowing that he would not answer; just continue staring.

Her eyes followed his gaze, she swallowed hard, and then steeled her will.

She started the car up again, forcing her ever-present anxiety back into its proper place as they moved through the remote, vaguely scenic countryside.

God, she hated being here. Until she saw the moors, it hadn't hit her just how much. But there was truly and utterly no other option. The bastard had abandoned her. And he hadn't just left their marriage, no. He'd left her with a steady amount of debt after completely destroying her credit. She couldn't afford their flat anymore, couldn't frankly afford much at all. And so now she had no option but to beg her mother to take her and Jeremy in until she got back on her financial feet.

Damn you, Reggie, she thought for the millionth time. *Scum-sucking pig!*

Sure, when Jeremy had been diagnosed, she'd heard a lot about parents of the disabled divorcing. But she'd never believed that would happen with her and Reggie. They were too mature, too understanding. They wouldn't let a little thing like autism get the better of them. And, hell, what was autism anyway? Nell herself was autistic and had handled it just fine, she told herself. Glancing out towards the moors now, she swallowed hard. Well, mostly fine, at least.

Yes, Jeremy's symptoms were severe. On a regular basis, he broke out into meltdown fits for three hours solid. Almost non-stop screaming. Most of the time, people had no idea what set him off and poor Jeremy, unable to speak a single word, had no means to convey the problem to them. To calm himself, he could only cover his ears with both hands and rock back and forth.

So many of the things that both parents had envisioned doing with their child…well, with Jeremy, those just hadn't been possible. Doctors said that his symptoms would likely lessen in time. Eventually, he would probably learn to talk and better handle the sensory overload constantly assailing him. But, for Reggie, eventually wound up being too far away.

"You can't leave," she'd protested back in London. "What about your son?"

"Let's be honest, for once!" Reggie had snapped. "The cold hard truth, Nell, is that he won't even notice I'm gone."

"How dare you. How dare you!" she'd shrieked. "He's got a brain, not a head full of sawdust. Of course, he'll bloody-well notice!"

"I don't think so," he'd replied stiffly. "I used to delude myself. I used to tell myself that it would be alright... But that kid has more in common with one of those robot baby dolls that they give randy teenagers to take care of for twenty-four hours as a warning against promiscuity than he does with a regular human. What's he do, eh? He screams, he organizes, and he stares. I can't take him to the park. I can't take him to the zoo. I can't watch a movie with him. I can't teach him how to play ball... Once people like you and me had options—"

"Options? You mean, back in the day, we could've just dumped him off in an institution and said, 'Hurray, he's not our problem now.'"

"Yes!" Reggie had roared. "I do mean that! Because I want a normal life and that kid ensures that's never going to happen. I wanted a son, not a lifelong sentence."

She'd slapped him then—hard. So hard his lip actually split. She'd never hit him before and still had a difficult time believing that she'd done it. She wasn't that kind of person. She wasn't violent. And yet…as she fully understood the gravity of all that Reggie was saying, she couldn't bring herself to feel any remorse for the action.

"Back in those old good days that

you're referencing," she'd spat, "I'd have been locked up in one of those institutions myself. And if you think that our son should spend his childhood in a psychiatric hospital, then you're right. You don't belong here. Get out!"

"I will. I will get out," he'd assured her, grabbing his suitcase. "And wherever I wind up, I'll get what I do deserve: a better marriage and children that are actually worth having."

"Yeah? Well, I hope you catch a nice dose of syphilis first! Hopefully, that'll take you down a peg or two."

The fight continued for a while. When Reggie had stormed out the door, slamming it behind him, Nell had gone into Jeremy's room. If he was distressed by the raised

84

voices, he certainly gave no sign of it. My Little Pony. That was his thing, of the 1980s vintage sort almost exclusively. Jeremy would spend hours oh-so-neatly lining up his substantial collection around the room. One of the things which Nell could do which pleased Jeremy the most was when, if one of the ponies was in need of a scrub or a hair-brushing, she would attend to it with a grooming kit that she had created. At those moments, Jeremy's eyes would widen and he would gaze directly at his mother. The fixed-up toy always brought the most beautiful smile to his face. He'd let Nell hug him then, maybe ruffle his hair, as he returned to his play.

True, Jeremy couldn't express himself, but that didn't mean that he was a proverbial mannequin. He had feelings, the same as anybody else, damn it! And hell, his life was hard. So very, very hard... Other children (and their parents too) shunned him. He'd never had a single friend to play with, not one confidant to take his problems too.

Where did he think his father was now? What did he think was happening when he saw everything in his flat being put into cardboard boxes? Nell had explained to him that they were moving, but what had that really meant to him? Had he even vaguely understood what she was saying? She had no way of knowing.

Nell didn't remember much from her own childhood. What little did come to her mind was almost always unpleasant, if not downright ugly. She knew that she'd always had the panic attacks. Anxiety—how it had ever-seemed to circle round her with the intensity of a constrictor snake! Many autistic adults had difficulty recalling their early years. Was there more to it than that? Nell didn't know and didn't care to either.

Many times, she'd heard of how, as a little girl, she'd often wandered away from home and wound up missing on the moors. Vaguely, she recalled that this had been the only place where she'd felt genuinely calm. She wasn't sure, in retrospect, how cognisant she'd truly been of the moors being forbidden to her or how dangerous they could be. Oh, but how clearly she did recall their sing-song pull to her, the way they lured her, foot by foot, closer… Locals had said that she had the nine-lived luck of a cat not to sink into one of the bogs. Her mother, Aggie, had thrashed the daylights out of her every time that she'd been found…

Nope. June Cleaver, Aggie wasn't. Nell didn't like visiting her or even phoning her. To have to come crawling to her now, begging for help… *Damn you, Reggie!* She thought again.

Before long, cold wind whipping against her face, she was knocking on her mother's door. As she waited, she looked around her surroundings. The mud-and-trash-surrounded house wasn't in great shape. The barn beside it looked even worse, with one of its doors only halfway still connected. Glancing down at Jeremy, Nell wondered if it was safe to still go inside.

After a few more knocks, the sixty-year-old woman made it to the door. "Hi, Mom," Nell put forward.

Aggie looked over her shoulder at the moving van attached to the back of the car—forehead wrinkling with a frown. "Hopefully, you won't be here long enough to unpack that."

"From your lips to God's ears," Nell agreed, trying not to sound as enthusiastic to leave as she truly was.

Begrudgingly, Aggie opened the door wide enough for the two of them to enter the house. Nell took a deep breath and instantly regretted it. The smell was terrible—not even from the general untidiness so much as the mould in the walls. She'd offered to help her mother deep clean the place before, but Aggie always refused. "I remember how you used to clean before you moved out of here. There's no way I'll go through that hell again."

Aggie wasn't entirely wrong. As a kid, it had been hard for Nell, almost impossible really, when she was scrubbing things down, to turn the water faucets off. She couldn't put her addiction to water rightly into words. Something about watching the liquid flow, hearing its slightly melodious gurgling, had entranced her, made all of life's yuckiness go away. The water bills had many times over reflected this obsession of hers and, many times over, this had repeatedly resulted in more brutal thrashings.

Nell knew that she shouldn't bring up the state of the house to her mother, but a few hours later, the words just slipped out over dinner. "Now that I'm here, Mom, I could help you get some stuff done around here."

"You should be spending your time looking for a job or finding someone to take care of the boy."

Nell blinked. She'd just assumed that—

"What? You didn't think that I was going to be doing that, did you? Nope, girl, that little squirt sitting next to you is your responsibility alone."

Nell placed her hand on Jeremy's shoulder, giving him a gentle squeeze. Reggie's mom was passed on, making Aggie the only grandmother he would ever know. Nell wholeheartedly wished that she had something better to give her boy than…than this!

"I don't suppose that you know anybody that you think is fit to look after him, once I do find employment?"

Aggie raised her eyebrows. "Actually, you are in luck there. The lady at the farm next door had a girl on the spectrum and, like you, she's down on her luck in a financial way. You take a walk over there tomorrow morning. Tell her who you are. I let her walk on my property every week, so there's no need to be too formal about the inquiry."

"Why has she been walking on the property?"

"There's an area in the moors that she frequents. It would be quite a hardship for her to go around this farm, so she has to make friendly with me. She's a bit on the emotional, high-strung side for my standards, but she does bake reasonably well. I don't mind the occasional cake or batch of Spudnuts left on my doorstep."

"You make her pay a toll?"

"I'm disinclined to allow trespassers. If she wants to pay me in goods, so be it. And frankly, my dear, you shouldn't judge me for the arrangement. If anything, I am far too lenient in tolerating her little excursions. It's only because I know how dangerous it is to take the long way around my farm that I let her pass through it. I suppose though that it's really only putting off the inevitable."

"Inevitable?"

"One of these days, she's going to go past my door up towards that spot of hers, take one wrong step, and never come back down again."

"Didn't you used to say that about me?"

"Yes," Aggie replied tightly. "And, given how many times you disappeared up there when you were little, to be blunt, I still don't know why you're alive."

Nell frowned, wishing she could remember more about it. Truth be told, she didn't even recall how she'd got out of the house so often. Hadn't anyone been watching her? Defensive as Aggie was, Nell knew better than to ask.

The next day, she followed her mother's instructions, travelling to the small farm of Alice Winchester, which lay in conditions not much better than her own mother's. "I'm Aggie Allred's daughter, Nell," she informed the woman, whose features were a little bewildered by a stranger's knock on the door. Nell understood her jumpiness. This part of the country was fairly remote and strangers weren't common. "Well, I just moved back here and my mother told me to inquire if you could be hired as a sitter. My boy's autistic and—"

"And so your mother sent you here?"

The woman's eyes enlarged, and her nostrils flared with automatic indignation.

"She told me that your daughter is—"

"Dead! My daughter's dead," she snapped. "Has been for almost a year. Children have no business being here, particularly autistic ones. They hear it too easily. Now, please, leave!" Sharply, she shut the door in Nell's face. Nell swallowed difficultly and squeezed Jeremy's hand.

What? What exactly did they hear? Nell blinked, feeling like she should understand the strange comment somehow...

Later that evening, she watched Jeremy as he stood at the window looking towards the moors. His hand stroked the glass repeatedly, as if he were desperate to get outside. "We'll go for a walk tomorrow, sweetie," she called to him. He looked back in her direction, though not exactly at her, and made a pleading, grunting noise.

Nell wondered if she ought to call her mother out on the obvious set-up she'd pulled. Ultimately, she decided against it. She wouldn't be baited by the old lady's nasty pranks. She'd just keep looking for a babysitter and wait for the right opportunity to apologise to Alice Winchester.

That opportunity came three days later, when Alice made her weekly trip past the house. Though Alice was speed walking (no doubt to avoid talking to anyone), Nell ran outside and quickly fell into step beside her. "Mrs Winchester," she started a little breathlessly. "I just wanted to say how sorry I am about the other day. I truly had no idea."

"I see."

"I truly apologise for upsetting you."

"It's not your fault that your mother didn't say anything."

"I'm sure that she meant to."

"Sure," Alice scoffed. "Sure, she did." She stopped in her tracks. "I meant what I said, you know: you really shouldn't have that little boy around here. As a former local, I'm sure that you know there's always been problems, but now...well...it's got a lot worse in recent years."

"What has?"

Alice blinked. "Surely, your mother must have warned you."

"Warned me about what?"

Alice frowned. "She is…watching him right now, isn't she?"

"No."

"Then what in God's name are you doing out here talking to me?" Alice near shrieked, marching back towards the house herself.

"Excuse me?"

"You can't leave that little kid alone."

"My son is still asleep."

"You don't know that! You aren't watching him right now. It doesn't take more than a minute or two and then, boom, your kid is gone. Believe me, I know!" Without asking, Alice stormed into the house in search of Jeremy. Only when she saw him in peaceful repose on the couch, large stuffed horse tucked under his arm, did she calm down. Hand over her heart, she took several deep breaths. "You don't know," she choked, looking back at Nell. "It's bad enough under normal circumstances. But autistic children, the way that they wander... The way that they have absolutely no sense of what is dangerous... They are so incredibly, incredibly innocent. And they can be taken advantage of, lulled by a predator with such ease." Alice's eyes fell back onto Jeremy's little face. "You are lucky. You have a beautiful child—one that is still alive; one that hasn't been taken. But you can't let your guard down, not even for a moment or he will be... All that I did was go to the bathroom. Maybe I was gone for two or three minutes, but not more than that. When I came out, my Susan had disappeared. She was eight. It took two months to find what was left of her."

Nell swallowed. "Did they catch who did it?"

"Not who, but *what*. And yes, everyone knows *what* did it. They think that it can't be caught. But it killed my daughter, so I will hunt it until the end of my days. That's what you do when you're a mother."

Nell shivered, afraid to ask the next question. "Exactly...what are you doing, coming through my mother's property every week?"

"The thing that killed Susan is out there." Alice pointed through the living room window at the moors. "It killed before her, will kill again after her if it's not stopped." Alice pulled her jacket back, revealing a gun. Nell clamped a fist in front of her mouth, gasping. "Maybe I can kill it. Maybe I can't. If I die trying, so be it," Alice shrugged.

"Is it...is it a big dog?"

"If only. That would've died up there in the bog a long time ago."

"Then what?"

Alice frowned. "How could your mother not tell you? Not even warn you?" She took a deep breath, shaking her head back and forth. "It's a grindylow."

Nell blinked and then cautiously

102

approached Alice, manoeuvring herself between this obvious madwoman and the slumbering child. "As I said, I am sorry to have upset you. But I think now it's best if you continue on your way."

Alice's shoulders slumped slightly. "Little ones are pulled to the marshes here. Susan wasn't the first, no—not by a long shot. And autistic children, more than others, are easy targets for the beast. Every autism parent in the world knows that autistic children are drawn to flowing water... It is why so many of them drown, even under typical circumstances. But here, this situation is anything but typical. Take that boy of yours and go back where you came from. It's the only way that he'll stay alive."

Not until the early morning hours could Nell sleep that night. As she stared at the ceiling in the darkness, there was no doubt in her mind that the creature that lurked in bogs, waiting like a crocodile, to pull children to their deaths was only a myth. And yet, something about Alice's desperation and sincerity left Nell's mind wandering. The more tired that she became, the more flashes of puddles, mud, and high grass sprung into her mind.

Drifting into sleep finally, Nell could almost remember how extremely frustrated her mother had been... Back in the 1980s, girls were almost never diagnosed with autism. One had to truly have extremely severe symptoms to merit the title. Aggie wasn't the kind of woman who would've been a loving, patient mother to a neurotypical child, but a disabled one…no, she absolutely had not signed up for that. And she resented terribly being forced to live with the added inconvenience and public stigma.

The time eventually came when Aggie decided to do something to increase what she considered her own quality of life... Aggie took her little daughter by the hand and led her up towards the bog. She didn't push her in. She just…let her go. And then she turned on her heels back in the direction of their house. She had no intention to watch what was going to happen next. Time after time before this, Aggie had led Nell away from their farm, but always, Nell had managed to find her way back. But on this occasion, with that water just ten or so feet away…little Nell was transfixed. She stared. On and on, she stared, unable to break her gaze away from the silent liquid song.

She took a step forward, a peaceful smile starting to spread across her features. The water didn't look very deep, with ample clumps of high grass sticking up out of it here and there. She only wanted to touch it, to run her fingertips across its cool, comforting surface. Reaching out a hand towards it, she took another step…and another…and another. She felt the soil beneath her boots start to give under her weight, just a little bit, but still she kept moving forward…until she saw it. The dead deer. So perfectly preserved was the poor creature underneath the bog's surface that, at first glance, it looked completely alive. And then Nell had noticed its leg emerging above the acidic water. That leg was long-denuded bone and nothing else, and it prompted her to let out a high-pitched, lengthy scream.

She turned to flee from the corpse and, as she did, the bog beneath her gave way. She was stuck! Frigid water came spilling into the tops of her knee-high boots, prompting another shriek. She struggled and, as she did so, she only seemed to sink more, almost up to her thighs. Nell tried to call out, "Mom!" But, more often than not, she couldn't talk at all. She was still learning. Would her pitiful pleas for help be loud enough for her now-disappeared parent to hear? As the bog seemed to only solidify its hold on her, she only could shriek and hope.

She lost her ability to stay standing, falling face first against a clump of vegetation. Thank God! There was some substance underneath it, perhaps a little bit more solid ground. She was able to keep herself from drowning.

She didn't hear the chuckling—not at first, at least. In the beginning, Nell was too overwhelmed by her own panic and the sound of her own sobs to notice the slight, sickening sound of amusement coming up closer and closer behind her. But finally, she did realize that she was not alone. She turned and then saw what no adult would believe, but every child knows to instinctively fear: a monster. It was about half her size, but in its spindly, green-skinned limbs it contained much more than twice her strength. Its bright eyes flashed with pleasure as it latched onto her boots, trying to pull her further into the water.

Still screaming, she fought, trying to kick it right in is devilishly sharp fangs. It could've yanked her into the depth with one single, swift motion, but it tugged slowly instead, enjoying her fear, delighting in her panic.

It had tricked her, she knew. From underneath the water, somehow it had lured her, all so that it could kill her. And for what purpose would it do that? Most likely, she assumed, to eat her. Unlike that deer, her body would never be seen again. Not a bone from her body, not a hair from her head, not a shred of her dress would remain once this creature had its way...

She gripped the vegetation, her only tie to actual land, with both tiny fists for dear life. The grindylow loosened its grip, making her think that she could escape, and then it seized hold of her tightly again. It did this several times, only laughing louder each time that her hopes were dashed. But then, it let her loose just for a few moments too long. She did manage to get one leg free and kick it hard in the face, sending its little body back into the muck a few feet away.

Nell knew this would be her last chance. With one desperate tug, she managed to finally yank herself out of the water onto the plants. Realising that its prey was getting away, the creature sprang into action, grabbing her again by the ankle. But the water-logged boot that she was wearing slid from her body. She found herself running. Only for a mere second did she look back to see the cursing, roaring grindylow throwing her boot down furiously into the bog...

Nell sat up with a start, gasping; barely even able to breathe. Panicked, she looked out of the darkened window in the direction of the moors. And then she looked towards her mother's bedroom.

It was a nightmare. Of course, it had to be. Grindylows didn't exist! But...had her mother actually been the one taking her up to the bog, leaving her to die? *Hoping* that she would die? All those thrashings that

Nell remembered her mother giving her, were they not for her wandering, but for her returning?

She stormed into her mother's bedroom, not hesitating, not even thinking of the consequences of asking such questions. "Alice told me that her little girl, Susan, drowned in the bog," she choked.

"Huh?" Aggie rubbed her eyes groggily. "What are you on about?"

"How could you be so heartless as to not tell me, while saying that she would want to babysit Jeremy?"

"I figured that she could use the money."

"No," Nell spat. "You sent me to her because her daughter died the way that you wanted me to die, didn't she? That's how horrible and sick you truly are! Her little girl was killed and it left you, what, reminiscing?"

Aggie sucked in her breath, eyes narrowing coldly. "I don't have to listen to this. I'm going back to sleep."

"You tried to murder me."

"Accidents!" Aggie snapped. "They happen to children all the time—stupid, dumb, defective children, in particular. It's nature's way of weeding out the undesirables."

"And that's what I was to you? An undesirable?"

"You were a mute, wilful thorn in my side! And you've given birth to another one just like you. Reggie was right, you know. When brats like that were put into institutions and it made things better for everyone. But, before the institutions, there were...other means. Children that were daft were simply..."

"What? Slaughtered?"

"It was done for the greater good." Aggie pushed herself up in bed, folding her arms defiantly over her chest. "Besides, there are worse ways to go than drowning. You liked the moors, didn't you? You liked the bog... I thought that it was the sort of place that you would've preferred to breathe your last in."

"Struggling in freezing water and mud? You thought that was a gentle death?"

Aggie didn't respond, only stiffened her lip.

"You're a monster," Nell whispered. "I truly never realised just how much of one until this moment. Alice said a grindylow killed Susan. Well, there's worse than grindylows. There's you and the vile bastards like you! Thank God, you don't have free rein to do whatever you want to children anymore in this society."

Aggie's eyes flared, but again she said nothing. Tears sliding down her face, Nell retreated from the room and began to gather up her things, loading them back up into the car outside. Finally, she picked up Jeremy, still sleeping, and carried him away. As she placed him into the back seat, she covered him with a blanket and set his box of toy horses beside him. She stroked his hair for a moment. God, she loved him.

He deserved better than this, and by God, he would have it. Would they have to live in a shelter for a while? Probably. Wherever they wound up, it would certainly be hard living. But he would be safe and that was all that mattered. Nell would never speak to Aggie again; Aggie would never know the wonderful young man that her grandson would one day become.

Nell wrote to Alice, explaining what had happened, how hearing of Susan's death had triggered her own memories. "I can't believe that the grindylow is real," she stated in the numerous subsequent letters exchanged between them. "Perhaps, given how long ago it was, my childish imagination simply transformed my mother's cruelty into the gruesome fantasy of a grindylow." In response, Alice only conveyed how glad she was that both Nell and Jeremy had managed to escape the fate that Susan had not.

Some years later, Alice stopped writing. Eventually, Nell googled her name. An online article from her hometown's newspaper quickly popped up. "Woman Discovered in Bog," it was titled. And there it was, the inevitable sad ending for a mother who would stop at nothing to avenge the loss of her daughter. She died, stuck in the mud, not from drowning, but from hypothermia. A slow, terrible death. Mysteriously, when she was found, she was clutching a gun, filled with empty rounds. What had she been firing at?

The police could only speculate and, indeed, given the presence of a child's leather boot in her other hand, the speculations were grim indeed.

Nell didn't sleep that night. Instead, she only stared at Jeremy, asleep in his bed. At one point, as if he sensed her, he opened his eyes, blinking in surprise. "Mom?" he asked. Yes, after extensive speech therapy, he could finally do that now. "Is everything okay?"

She didn't know how to respond. Could a grindylow even bleed? Could it be killed? Had Alice's miserable final moments been successful?

Nell smiled, nodded unconvincingly, and returned to her own bedroom. She felt very small at that moment, as if she were still in the bog, trapped and struggling against the terrible, slime-covered, verdant creature. Perhaps, in some ways, she still was. Perhaps she always would be.

First published in *Mythica*, Iron Faerie Publishing, 2020

BLACK HARE PRESS

THE HUNTING CABIN

By Jacqueline Moran Meyer

I wake up in the basement of my hunting cabin.

Mark, my childhood friend, and I came here for our annual hunting trip, two years ago, and never went home. We only leave the cabin to hunt but haven't travelled beyond the nearest town.

On a brilliant autumn day, with the shock of red and yellow leaves shining in the bright sun, the world ended. We were eating breakfast when the ground shook, followed by a loud boom rattling our eardrums. The sky darkened into a perpetual cold grey twilight. We drove to the nearest town and learned a meteor fell in Brazil. We looted the market with town residents and went back to the cabin and stayed, living on water from the well and food we caught. Soon the plants and trees turned black. Frozen ash fell from the purple cloud-covered sky like papier mâché. We snapped off branches and crumbled them into my wood stove for fuel. We stayed warm, but quickly exhausted our food supply.

The hunger drove us insane. We rationalised raiding the nearby town as the only way to survive. We walked into empty homes and opened barren cabinets. In the last home we entered Mark heard whispers coming from the basement. The stench assaulted us, we retched after we opened the basement door. We found a small family of four living amongst the gore of human remains—the same family displayed in the pretty frames upstairs. Mark described the family as our saviours. I can't bear to describe them. How can one describe live food? It is like describing a lobster you have picked out of a tank for dinner. They had to look ugly, pitiful, weak. Mark convinced me we needed to rid ourselves of competition stealing our resources.

We took them back to the cabin and after a few weeks we laid the last of the butchered meat into the frozen earth. We ate; our strength and hope grew.

Inevitably, starvation pangs came again when we finished the meat. I suggested we go hunting in town. Mark nodded but didn't look me in the eye. He hadn't been speaking to me much. I should have seen this coming; he is the stronger of the two of us, needed more food. He attacked me in bed last night and threw me down the stairs into the basement. I am not dead, yet. If I can knock through the door and walk up the stairs maybe I can grab my rifle. I have one bullet left and can either shoot him or run into the town and hunker down in one of the abandoned houses.

I try to bring myself to my feet but wince in pain. My right foot is useless, broken. Stifling a cry, I crawl over to the door dragging my leg behind me. The cabin is quiet. I pull myself up and wrap my hand around the doorknob. A jolt of excitement runs through me as I find it unlocked. I peer up. Mark stands, laughing before he pulls the trigger.

A TASTE FOR FLESH

By L.P. Hernandez

The sun was like poison on his skin. He turned away from the window, but the room filled with light, and he was now fully awake. He wished he could sleep for a week, a month, wrap himself in a cocoon and emerge as a transformed man.

His head.

Nothing in his thirty-two years compared to the pain he felt in his head. If there had been a gun on the nightstand instead of a cheap alarm clock, he would have added the grey matter of his brain to the puddle of sweat on the pillow.

His body was a wreck.

He tried to think, but each thought was a corkscrew, twisting and turning within his skull. He willed his trembling hands to his temples, which pulsed like a hummingbird's wings.

The stash.

It was old, many years old by now, but it was something.

Adam stood on brittle legs, a sunbaked

scarecrow at the end of summer. The floor heaved and rolled beneath his bare feet, and he held out his arms as if walking a tightrope. Swaying and stumbling, the bile in his belly crawled up his throat.

Adam and his father visited the cabin throughout his childhood. They were some of his earliest and clearest memories. Days spent fishing on the lake. Nights around a campfire with bubbling marshmallows slumping at the end of a charred twig.

Now, the cabin was his prison.

"I'll be back in a week, son. It's the only way."

The next sound was of tires crunching over dirt and gravel.

But his father did not know Adam had been sick for a long time. Half his life by then.

He staggered out of the bedroom into the hallway.

The stash. It was somewhere in the cellar.

Adam fell to his knees and cast aside the threadbare rug that covered the trapdoor leading into the cellar. His fingers quivered as they sought the iron ring. What his father did not understand was this was not a choice for him. The fingers, straw-thin and weak, fumbled with the cold metal.

Sweat collected below his hairline, though it was not particularly warm in the cabin. Adam's fingers gripped the iron ring, and he straddled the trapdoor. The hinges shrieked as he wrenched it open.

Cool, putrid air gusted up from the cellar. Adam turned his head to the side and vomited. It was mostly stomach acid but had the consistency of a raw egg and was similar in colour.

How long had it been since the cellar door was opened? Half a decade?

The steps descended into darkness. A single lightbulb hung in the centre of the room, but Adam would need to walk into the shadows to find it. He placed his bare foot onto the wood of the first step. It felt slick beneath his rough soles, and he rubbed his hands together as he considered his next move.

Adam glanced at the door. He could make a run for it. He knew the way, but it was a long way. The nearest paved road was fifteen miles as the crow flies. It was not easy going, either. In his condition he would end up in a ravine wishing he was back in this goddamned cabin, stash or no stash.

The wood sagged beneath him. He grimaced, willing himself to be lighter somehow. Adam redistributed his weight, holding himself up with the floorboards as he descended beneath the house.

There were no windows, just an elongated slab of light from the living room. Beyond the borders of that light, little could be seen. The pain, the cold spike in his brain sprouted icy capillaries into his muscles. For the second time in the ten minutes since he woke, Adam wished he was dead.

He reached the bottom, feet slipping over the bare earth. In the shadows there were mason jars filled with canned tomatoes, okra, and other vegetables that spoiled years ago. He could not see them, but he knew they were there, and the stash was hidden among them. He hoped.

Adam flinched. His subconscious mind registered the sound, and his fingers curled into fists. He found the cord he sought and tugged. The light bulb fizzled and hissed before casting a reluctant yellow glow in a small circle around him.

The earth glittered, reflecting glints of light. Adam frowned, brows knitted in confusion. Then he noticed the bare shelves. The jars were gone. All except two or three tipped on their sides. Perhaps his father finally disposed of them. Adam always believed stockpiling Mom's canned vegetables in the cabin was just Dad's way of avoiding having to eat them.

He looked from the shelves to the floor and whispered, "Shit…"

The mason jars were rubble, their contents evaporated or…

"Shit!" he shouted, retreating a step.

Glass crunched beneath his left foot, but the pain could not compete with the fire and ice wreaking havoc on his muscles. The rat lingered beyond the reach of the light, a smudge of grey against a black backdrop. At once, Adam was transported to a dozen nameless alleys and overpasses. His heartbeat quickened, body itching from the memories of rat bites. He once woke to find one nursing at a sore in the crook of his elbow, sipping his polluted blood and tearing away tiny strips of grimy flesh.

He eyed the intact jars and knew they would not contain what he sought, what he needed. Adam crouched, searching the shadows for a hint of the rat's shape. His finger traced the reptile skin of his arm. It was the rats that drove him out of the city, to his childhood home where his weakness was exposed. It was the rats that nudged the mason jars off their reliable perches, seeking the sustenance within.

His fingers found only glass. There was movement to his right, another rat. If there was one, there would be more. Tears cascaded through the weathered canals of his cheeks. His father did not know this experiment would not save him. It would kill him.

He crawled to the second shelf, equally devastated by the rats. Only, here there was no light, not even a hint of it. Glass fragments carved divots out of his knees and bored into his palms. His fingers grazed something furry and he screamed.

It was a rat corpse, partially eviscerated. Foul beasts. Unforgivable beasts, eating their own.

Adam probed the detritus.

"Come on. Come on."

More glass and dirt. His stomach twisted, threatening to add its contents to the vile collection he could not see.

"Come on," he whispered again.

And then, a miracle. Paper. A small

envelope and the ice in his brain dissipated for a moment, projecting the respite to come. He hid the stash here years ago, maybe knowing a day such as this would happen. Adam stood and brushed the glass from his hands and knees.

He walked to the circle of light and examined the envelope. It would not get him high. But, he was not looking to get high. He was only interested in delaying his suffering.

Adam turned his head at the sound of chattering. He tapped the light bulb and it swung, casting light into a dark corner of the room. In flashes he saw her, a fat rat, the fattest he'd ever seen. Half a dozen or more tiny, pink rats suckled from her swollen teats.

A mischief of rats. The word came to him from somewhere, a high school textbook maybe, or a long ago game of Trivial Pursuit with his father.

He snickered, then noticed the blood on his hands and knees. It was the rats. It was always the rats. Adam seized one of the intact mason jars, aimed, and hurled it toward the bloated, nursing mother. The glass shattered and was followed by a squeal of pain. The light bulb's motion slowed, and Adam was unable to view the result of his handiwork.

***

There was not enough to ration. That is what he told himself. There were also no syringes, so it was not even a clean hit. Adam had to get creative, but that was a natural talent for someone with his history.

Cold rain battered the windows. It was an early autumn storm, one Adam and his father would have enjoyed from the comfort of the porch in his previous life. He lay on the couch, the blood on his knees and palms crusted over but the wounds not yet scabbed.

As predicted, he was not high, but the pain was tolerable for the moment. Adam had no future plan beyond searching the cellar for another miracle, though he knew there was nothing to be found. Past Adam would never sacrifice more than one dose for future Adam.

Between rumbles of thunder, he drifted to sleep. He dreamed only of the next fix, of how good it would feel not to hurt. One rat emerged from the open cellar door followed by two others. In the cold room below the mother rat kicked in her death throes. All but one of her pups was still. The survivor nursed from her ruined body as her life soaked into the earth.

More rats scaled the steps, some in pursuit of food, others following the scent trail of the man now sleeping on the couch. They were mostly thin with slick, matted fur in shades of midnight. Their naked tails, adorned with sparse, fibrous hairs, drew wavy patterns in the dust on the floor.

Still more rats scampered out of the darkness as Adam cradled his stomach and turned on his side. His arm hung limp, the knuckles grazing the floor. He twitched in his sleep, unaware of the audience assembling around him.

The dead mother rat birthed dozens of babies in her years. Some moved on, leaving the safety of the cabin's cellar through a network of tunnels to explore the vast wilderness beyond its walls. Many others remained as faithful servants, venturing into tall grass outside to forage, returning to share their spoils.

In Adam's dream, he held a lighter beneath a spoon. He licked his dried, broken lips, anticipation building. This would be enough to make him feel something, to quiet the pain and bring him to the precipice of bliss. A tendril of black smoke twisted in a thin ribbon, the spoon's contents just beginning to sizzle.

Dream Adam dropped the spoon, not

accidentally. Dream Adam held a finger above the lighter's flame. The anticipation of pleasure usurped by pain. Dream Adam watched the skin blister.

He screamed himself awake. The rat darted under the couch and held within its sharp, yellowed teeth a morsel of flesh. It was evening somehow; the feeble grey light illuminated little. Adam held his hand in front of his face and squinted. A bit of bone peeked through the gore, and half his fingernail was gone.

"What the f—"

Adam scanned the room, his rheumy eyes probing the shadows. He sensed movement but was unable to focus on it. The rats were everywhere. The floor was alive.

Fine hairs brushed against the bare skin of his leg, and he screamed again, tumbling off the couch to the floor. He low-crawled out of the room, stood, and lumbered to the front door. It was late in the evening, the setting sun hidden behind a shapeless wall of clouds. Icy pinpricks of rain stung his face as he bounded off the porch.

Adam held his throbbing finger to his chest. There was nowhere to go. The silhouettes of tall trees leaned over him, and the gravel road disappeared into darkness. The clearing where he and Dad bonded over s'mores was overgrown, the lawn chairs slowly dismantled by nature.

He willed headlights to emerge from the dark. But, they did not come. He was alone.

There was nowhere to go but back inside with the rats. The rain needled the nape of his neck as he lowered his head, returned to the porch and climbed the rotting steps. He closed the door behind him and turned on the light.

They fled to darkness, moths in reverse. They huddled under the furniture, chittering, spreading rumours. Adam's body was rigid, the muscles taut and twitching. He stepped onto the linoleum floor of the small kitchen, eyes dancing from one collection of shadows to the next.

The cabin was tiny, its sources of light few. Adam flipped on every light switch, and the rodents fled before him. He peered into the darkness of the cellar before slamming its door closed.

Rust-coloured water spat out of the faucet in spurts. Adam pinched the tip of his bloodied finger and waited. He sensed the rats watching him, felt the weight of their beady black eyes, the tireless desire of their rancid teeth. Whatever comfort the hit brought him leaked out of his body, exiting via the ragged stump at the end of his finger.

The water cleared and he held his finger beneath it. It was icy cold, which intensified the pain. He would leave tomorrow. Even if the journey killed him, it was better than this place. He would be a failure in his father's eyes, at least for another day. Surely his father would prefer a living failure to the alternative.

He wrapped his finger in a dish towel and sagged against the counter. This place was trapped in time. Hand-me-down decorations and furniture raided from sidewalks in well-to-do neighbourhoods. His mother's cross-stitch atrocities hung from brass hooks here and there. He scratched his neck with his free hand.

There were too many memories here. They disputed the frenzied assurances of his chaotic mind. He had been happy once, unaided. The sight of a shooting star sent him floating. The hoot of an owl sent his imagination reeling. His father's rough hands helping him to bait a hook. The still waters of the lake as they watched their red and white bobbers. The sound of breakfast sizzling in an iron skillet.

At the centre of it all, was his father.

Adam shook his head.

Not now.

He left the kitchen for the bathroom. There were few hiding places there. After a quick inspection, Adam decided it was safe to shower. That was what he needed. A warm shower and maybe a snack after.

As in the kitchen, the faucet sputtered and gurgled, spraying the tub with dirty water. He waited for the water to clear and caught sight of himself in the mirror. It was the closest to sober he had been in months, maybe years.

A stranger looked back at him. The stranger turned its face this way and that. Who was this man? Whose pitted cheeks? Whose moon-wide eyes? He pawed at his face, the unintended beard flecked with grey.

Adam hardly knew him. The stranger smiled, displaying whitened gums and butter-coloured teeth. The stranger frowned and turned away.

Scratching at the door.

The rats.

Adam turned the lock and stared at it, as if expecting the handle to jiggle. It was nearly night. He only needed to make it until the morning.

***

Dressed in the same clothes, battered blue jeans and a plain white T-shirt stiff and yellowed with sweat, Adam huddled under the blanket. He shared this bed with his father dozens of times over the years.

But now it was only him.

He shivered, teeth clattering so forcefully he feared the enamel might shatter. Nausea passed through him in waves, from head to toe and back up again. If he had anything other than bile in his stomach he would have vomited it. Instead, he gagged and spat over the side of the bed.

"Dad…"

He wished his father was with him and was also relieved the man would never have to see his son so low. So pathetic.

Adam peeled his head from the pillow. More scratching at the door.

He gathered the energy to scream, but whimpered instead, and burrowed deeper beneath the blankets. It smelled, faintly, of his father's musk, a combination of sweat and aftershave. He inhaled it, held it in his lungs, and felt his heartbeat slow.

Adam's nerves were on fire. He wanted nothing more than to leap from his own skin, to excavate his consciousness from his body. Yet, in the midst of his suffering there was the faintest beginning of hope. There was no possibility of a fix within these walls, and so his mind drifted elsewhere. He reached an arm across the bed to the place his father typically occupied. Though the man was not there, Adam found comfort in the knowledge he once had been.

The rain was a steady drone, like a box fan right next to his face. Hidden within it was the scratchy sound of a dozen rats biting into the wood of the bedroom door.

Adam fell asleep thinking about his father, but he dreamed only of rats.

***

Adam rode a wave of frenzied bodies. He opened his eyes and saw nothing. It was not darkness but blindness. And he was sinking. He kicked and crawled, and his body slipped further and further into the mass of rats, nipping and biting his skin.

They smelled of urine and faeces, of rotten meat liberated from the bottom of a restaurant's dumpster. They were up to his chest, and his arms became trapped. He opened his mouth to scream but only managed to bark in surprise as a rat began wrestling with his tongue. This was joined by another, who wedged itself in the warm, wet embrace of Adam's throat. Smaller rats plugged his nostrils with their horrid, blunted tails.

With each attempted breath, the rat wriggled deeper into his throat. They came for his eyes next, seizing them and thrashing their heads. Amid the pain and panic, he felt the warm pulp of his perforated eyeballs trickle down his cheeks.

Adam sat up in bed, clawing at his neck. His hair was pasted to his forehead. He blinked, caught between the reality of the bedroom and the sea of rats from his nightmare.

It tickled in his throat, and he gagged. Adam cinched his fist into a pincer and opened his mouth. He probed the back of his throat with dirty fingers, coughing and sputtering, eyes tearing. He withdrew a small collection of wiry hairs, not his own.

His stomach twisted and rolled.

"No," he said, removing his shirt.

There was just enough light in the room to see movement beneath the skin.

"No!"

He jumped out of the bed and stepped on a rat's tail. The rat screeched and sank its incisors into Adam's heel. He tripped and skidded, flattening another rat beneath his foot.

"No!" he screamed as he ran into the hallway.

Adam punted a rat as he entered the kitchen. It hit the far wall and collapsed onto the tiles. He cast aside his shirt and probed his belly. A rat was inside of him, carving into the soft tissue of his stomach. And if it was, what could he do? Vomit it up? Punch it from the outside?

But, there was no rat, no movement. His stomach was still and the sensation passed. The adrenaline in his body tapered off and he stood, panting in the kitchen.

The rat he'd kicked mewled in pain, drawing Adam's attention that direction.

"You bastard," he said.

Adam glanced around the room, then smiled when he spotted it. The cinderblock his father used to prop the front door open. Adam grunted as he hoisted it to chest-height.

"You rat bastard," Adam said, standing over the broken animal.

It pawed and kicked at the air, its tail

flicking uselessly. The memory of the nightmare was fresh in Adam's mind, the sensation of the rats invading his mouth and blocking his airway.

He lifted the cinderblock over his head, which required all of his strength to achieve. As he slammed the cinderblock down he screamed, exorcising the rage and frustration that dwelled like a toxin in his bones.

The rat exploded from both ends, ejecting its innards across the tiles. Adam did not have time to enjoy the moment. The rotted floorboards beneath the tiles caved in, and the rat corpse, cinderblock, and the man crashed through to the basement.

The cinderblock sank into the earth first. Adam followed behind, his body twisting so that it was perpendicular to the ground. He landed on his side, his neck colliding with the sharp edge of the cinderblock.

The pain was not immediate. Adam blinked a few times, unable to process the preceding moments. He reached an arm out. He attempted to reach an arm out, but the arm did not obey. The legs did not obey.

The pain in his body was different now. Adam's head rested on the cinder block, his neck wrapped around it in an L-shape. Blood purled from his lips, which seemed to be the only thing he was capable of moving other than his eyes.

Realisation came slowly. He could not feel his chest rise and fall. He did not know if he was breathing.

The rats initially scattered from the commotion now approached, tentatively, sniffing at the limp body. They smelled his sweat, his sickness, and his blood. More rats emerged from the darkness. Adam spotted half a dozen approach and could not scream. His eyes widened, and that was the only outlet for his terror.

In his mind he saw his arms flailing, battering the rodents. He pushed himself off the ground to tower over them. But this did not happen. He could only blink. He could only twitch his lips a little, like the rats twitched their whiskers.

As his body adjusted to its new condition, some of the feeling returned to his extremities. First his fingers, and then his toes. Little tingles, like the needle-sharp rain from the evening before. He focused all of his thoughts toward moving a finger. He closed his eyes and pictured it happening.

In that moment, he would have traded any amount of small, paper envelopes for the ability to move again. No temporary bliss compared.

Adam imagined his father opening the front door, seeing the ruin of the kitchen floor, and saving him from this place. It would have been some satisfaction to see the guilt in his father's eyes, but he really only wanted to see him again.

When he opened his eyes, he did not see his father. He saw a rat. The rat was sickly, its nose chewed to shreds during some previous altercation, likely with one of its kin. It inched forward, and dipped its mouth to the pool of blood spreading from between Adam's lips.

It was then Adam realised the tingling sensation was not the feeling returning to his limbs. He could not see them, could not move at all. But he knew.

They congregated around his fingers and toes, nipping the flesh there. As the skin broke and blood began to flow, their desire became a need. More and more rats emerged from the shadows, drawn by the scent of blood in the air. Some were the offspring of the mother rat, and their feeding was rooted in revenge. Others were merely hungry.

Adam felt all of it. He felt one hundred morsels of his flesh ripped from his body.

He felt the warmth as arteries were punctured and blood began to flow.

The rat with the disfigured nose, thirst satisfied, came for the flesh. It began with the lips, which jerked reflexively from the bites. It was joined by others less reserved in their need. They tore into the flesh of his cheeks, stripped the skin of his eyelids. He could no longer blink, no longer close his eyes. The last thing he saw, before his vision was taken from him, was yellowed rat teeth, dripping with his blood.

REVOLUTIONARY HUNGER

By Matthew M. Montelione

27 May 1784.
Southampton, New York.

Elijah Lockwood was confused, panting alone in a dark wood. He was incredibly hungry, feeling as if his stomach was withered. Indeed, he had not feasted for hours, being on the run from cruel men who chased him all over the countryside and into the forest.

**

Elijah was once a well respected man in his community. He wore only the finest suits, his favourite ensemble consisting of a vibrant red coat, a matching waistcoat and breeches, and a white silk cravat. He was the only son of the wealthy John and Mary Lockwood, who rose to prosperity in the 1750s thanks to John's savvy mercantile skills.

The family imported and sold a great amount of madeira wine, salt, duck, and lead and shot, among other popular English items. John made wealthy and influential friends, who supplied him with additional outlets of revenue. The Lockwoods became one of the richest families on Long Island. Although John was beloved in his community, he was not the most patient or compassionate father. He was coarse in speech and intolerant of failure.

Mary Lockwood, on the other hand, was generous, amiable, and caring. She was certainly the more reasonable, loving parent—firm when she needed to be, but never unkind. Elijah relied on her for sound advice, and to him, it seemed as though she never failed in giving the profoundest words of wisdom.

Since his birth, Elijah was groomed to inherit his father's position as a merchant. The younger Lockwood learned his duties rather well and was excited to be involved in his father's employ. Like his father, Elijah made important friends, and forged solid business connections. As he matured, he proved to be more popular than John; his personality was more akin to his mother's than his father's. It was not long until he had many clients thirsting for fine wines and meats.

Business was interrupted in the 1770s, when royal troops spilt colonial blood in Boston, igniting the American Revolution. The Lockwood family, having strong economic ties to the mother country, became firm Loyalists, vowing to fight for the Crown.

In 1776, Elijah reluctantly enlisted in a Loyalist regiment. His head wanted to fight, but his heart was torn in two. He loved Abigail Smith, the miller's daughter, and was planning on asking for her hand until the war broke out.

In August, Elijah fought alongside redcoats against the Continentals on western Long Island. He was not certain that his musket shot felled many enemies, it was hard to tell in the blur of blood, death, and screams of war. In early September, Elijah wrote to his parents and Abigail that he was well, training at a western camp. He was sure that he would be granted permission to visit home sometime in October.

The Lockwoods delighted in the good news and waited patiently for their son to return. When October came and passed without a word from Elijah, they grew concerned.

John wrote to Colonel Richard Hewlett, inquiring about his son's whereabouts. In mid-November, on a cold stormy night, he received the colonel's reply. Elijah was given leave to visit Southampton, having departed camp in early October. In the letter, Richard expressed his concern over Elijah's wellbeing, but also questioned his resolve, noting that a few young men had recently deserted.

John sneered at the accusation about

his son's character, throwing the letter into the roaring fire. He resolved to set out in search of his son.

During the night before his departure, John heard the wild and sudden neighing of his horses in the stables. Slipping on his coat, he lit a candle and went outside to investigate. As he approached the stable, he noticed its doors were half-open.

Candlelight exposed the dark figure of Elijah, huddling in the corner.

"Son!" John cried out, running over to him. The father's thrill turned to worry once he noticed the condition of his son.

Elijah was unshaven, his hair unkempt, his eyes looked sullen and yellowish. He was caked all over with what looked like a mix of blood, mud, and general grime.

"Hello, father," Elijah dully said.

"What has befallen you?"

Elijah stared blankly at John for a few moments before answering. He was clearly in some sort of shock. "I…I don't remember. I know I was attacked by a group of rebels in the woods of Mastic… Somehow, I fought them off. Killed one of them, the others took off."

John looked at his son with pity. "Come inside, son. It's cold out here. We'll discuss this over a drink near the fire. Your mother is going to be so relieved to see you. Our hearts have been strained since you went missing. We feared the worst."

"Mother," Elijah muttered. "Yes, I must see my mother. Then, I will see

Abigail."

"Abigail?" John asked, flashing his son a peculiar glance. "What does that miller's daughter have to do with you?"

At that, Elijah stood up tall in front of his father, breathing heavily. His eyes grew larger and brighter, his slow, lethargic countenance turned aggressive.

Mary opened the door and saw her son. "Elijah!" she cried, weeping tears of joy.

Elijah turned to his mother, and, upon seeing her, slowed his breathing, calming down.

Mary rushed over to him and walked her damaged son into the dimly lit house.

To the dismay of his parents, Elijah's memory was extremely scattered after his return. Military officers noticed his unstable state, relieving him of his duties in 1777. The American Revolution ended in 1783 without his participation; the British army was eradicated from the colonies.

Elijah withdrew from the family business, shunning his responsibilities. He grew more distant from everyone he loved, including Abigail. In the daylight hours, he frequented the church graveyard, praying next to random tombstones. When people spoke to him, his speech was often jumbled and confused. At night, he was nowhere to be found, although some of the townsfolk claimed that they saw him aimlessly roaming the countryside.

John and Mary tried their hardest to help Elijah, but their attempts were fruitless. John grew disgusted and restless.

In late 1783, he threw his son out of the house. Abigail, for her part, still loved Elijah. She had heard of men coming back from war changed in unusual ways. Was this some result of Elijah's experiences in battle? It drove her mad that she did not know exactly what had come to pass. She kept her distance, watching Elijah from afar, writing to him often. But deep down, Abigail started to realize that, if Elijah did not start acting like a functional member of society, she would begrudgingly have to move on from him.

For all of Elijah's shortcomings, he was keen enough to understand Abigail's position, and it drove him mad.

***

Elijah remained tormented and

confused in a dark wood on 27 May 1784. He started convulsing, losing control of himself again. His eyes yellowed, he screamed in anguish to the heavens. He heard the footsteps of his assailants coming closer and closer. They would soon be upon him. It was time to fight or flee, yet again. In truth, Elijah did not wish to hurt any more people. But now, reddened with rage at the thought of losing Abigail, he was tired of running. After all, he was much stronger and faster than his irritating pursuers. He smirked with sharpened teeth, giving in to his new nature.

The brutes, armed with farming tools, clubs, daggers, and muskets, stopped in their tracks when they reached him.

In Elijah's place stood a nightmarish

sight. He had become a wolf man in a fine red suit. He had the anatomy of a man but was no longer wholly human. Elijah's head looked like a large grey wolf's, and his body was covered with dark grey fur. His eyes pierced through the hearts of the once determined mob. The wolf man's mouth watered, snarling and gnashing his teeth. He pounced on one of the men and tore into his face. He felled three more assailants; the rest ran for their lives. Elijah the werewolf smiled as they fled, fresh flesh and blood dripping from his mouth. He was no longer hungry.

***

Epilogue.
[THURSDAY, JUNE 23, 1785].
THE NEW-YORK JOURNAL.

SOUTHAMPTON.

This past Sunday, the corpse of Mr John Lockwood was found in a most vile state near the shores of the beach. Parts of his flesh were torn off his body. The mangled condition of the merchant's corpse matches that of other victims who have been found in those accursed parts in recent years. Some people said that a demon with the face of a wolf terrorises the town and is responsible for the grisly deaths, but most believe that to be pure superstition. The murderer has not been captured.

First published in *Issue 8, Horror Bites Magazine*, October 2018

THE JAR

By McKenzie Richardson

They thought of her as a simple girl, a beautiful slave to her own curiosity. They trusted her with a jar, told her not to open it. What fools they'd been.

She lifted the lid and the plagues emerged, black as a raven's wing, scuttling along her elegant limbs. A grin snaked its way onto her face at their tickled promises of havoc.

Some were long and slug-like, slime seeping through oily skin, oozing as they slipped to the ground. They left trails of sinister sludge as they ventured forth, seeking the soft tissues of eye sockets that provided easy access to blacken minds.

Others took flight, coal-dark wings clicking a song of devastation. Their ebony shells shone as they skittered around her head, sending her hair whirling in dark tendrils. These creatures preferred the taste of human hearts, burrowing deep into chest cavities to infest and feast.

Illness, Anger, Hate, Greed, Suffering—they scattered and invaded every corner of the earth, rolling out like a cloud of death, afflicting all they touched. They sucked the world dry of goodness, then lapped up the resulting carnage.

She couldn't help it; she cackled in delight as mayhem ensued.

A soft voice sounded from the bottom of the jar where a pale light glowed. She sneered down at the thing still inside that asked so politely to be let out. Instead, she snapped the lid shut, keeping Hope locked up tight inside the crypt-like chamber. The beautiful girl, that mother of evils, stood tall, overseeing the bloodshed and chaos. There was no need for such brightness in this land.

History would remember her name, this bringer of destruction.

Give the world a pretty jar and they'll place it on the mantel. They'll never suspect the evil that lurks inside, waiting to creep out into the world, to shape it in its own image.

THE HARVEST

By Nerisha Kemraj

Marsha continued to rally the chickens into the coop after trying for twenty minutes. It was no easy feat, but it had to be done. In a few hours, if not before, the others would be here for their first harvest.

It was almost a year since they moved in, but the harvest was an old tradition.

She would have to hurry to gather all the other animals into their respective dens. Walking to the other side of the yard, she noted two familiar vehicles parked behind the old barn.

Seemed like Beth and David, along with Mr and Mrs Haversham, had already arrived. *Perhaps they caught up with Jake and his tractor as he left*, she thought, and she hurried to finish up rounding the animals. She'd see them soon enough, but she had to freshen up before then.

Feint screams stemming from above jolted her out of thought. Within seconds, the yelling got closer. Straining to see against the sunlight, she made out the form of her husband. Jake dangled from the tail of a huge snake-like creature. Massive wings flapped on each side, causing a cloud of dust to swirl around her. She figured she must've been dreaming, but a drop of blood fell onto her ashen face as the thing swooped down into the barn. Large emerald eyes, the size of her hand, glowered at her as they passed. Jake's piercing screams rang through the air, and she caught sight of his blood-drained face before it disappeared into the barn. His tractor was nowhere to be seen.

She stood frozen for a few minutes until the frightened cows broke her out of her shock as they rampaged through the yard. What had she just seen? She rubbed her eyes—it must have been her imagination. But the ruckus of the other animals told her otherwise.

She rushed to grab the shotgun from inside the house, not knowing how useful it would be against a creature of that size, but knowing that it was what she had to do.

She bumped into Old John, dropping him to the ground, as the shotgun fell from her hands. There was no sign of the others.

"Sorry, Old John! I'm sorry, I have to get Jake." She extended her hands helping him to his feet, astounded by her own calmness, and grabbed the gun before making a mad dash towards the barn.

"What's going on?" Old John shouted after her.

"Something took Jake! An enormous flying creature with green eyes!" She paused. I *must be going crazy*, she thought.

John swore under his breath as he ran towards his van. To anyone else, Marsha would've sounded like someone who belonged in the Looney Bin…but John didn't need to be told twice. This was it. He clutched at the scar across his chest – the one given to him by the same beast years ago. After ten years, the creature was back to feast, just as it had done for hundreds of years. But this time he was ready. It took many months for him to work out the exact day of its arrival, but he had done it…and now here it was. He grabbed the gun with its box of gold-plated bullets—the only thing that worked against the beast. This time there would be no harvest for that monster.

Marsha cocked the shotgun, ready to shoot. The smell of iron hit her as she entered the barn. Scrunching her nose, she gagged at the sight before her. Jake, unconscious now, was suspended in the air, the tail of the dragon-like creature pierced through his abdomen as blood gushed onto the floor like water from an opened tap. The bloody, lifeless bodies of the Havershams, Beth and David, all hung from the rafters. They were cocooned with a thin veil, like the one that the creature now spun around Jake, using its spit as thread, to wrap him up.

Marsha fired a shot at it, causing it to let out an angry roar as it lunged towards her, dropping Jake to the ground. Ducking just in time, she managed to fire another shot at it. But the bullets were of no use as it bounced off its scales. The raging beast cornered Marsha just as Old John arrived, throwing a spear towards the creature. Snarling at him, the beast turned his eyes away from Marsha, it was just enough time for her to break into a run as the spear struck it in the eye. But Marsha was not quick enough. Growling in agony it clawed at the spear stuck in its eye, thrashing about wildly. Just then, Old John fired off a shot as Marsha cried out in pain when its flailing claws dug into her. Goop-like jelly rained down around the barn as bullets tore through its majestic scales. Anguished wails echoed through the barn, and it swung its tail, striking Old John across his chest. He fell to the ground, grabbing his gun he fired another round of bullets into the face of the fast-approaching monster. It fell to the ground with a thunderous thud while John ran towards Marsha, but it was too late. The beast's claws remained lodged in her chest as they both breathed their last.

THE TEMPEST ON THE PIER

By Pedro Iniguez

Robert Tapia rubbed his frizzled chin and stared at the dark waters below. The waves crashed against the pillars of the pier, spraying foamy white mist into the air.

He stuffed a cigarette into his mouth and lit up, inhaling a stream of hot fumes. He coughed violently as the fire in his lungs flared. His tongue tasted wet copper on his cracked lips.

The sun was sinking below the horizon and the November breeze kicked up, blowing Robert's hoodie away from his head. He had picked the tip-end of the pier for tonight. He found that spot was always the most appealing, being the farthest from society one could possibly be and the closest to the ocean without being in any real danger.

San Clemente, California—a small beach town of quaint shops, twinkling lights, the clearest skies in all of Southern California. It's where Robert's father had taken him time and again to teach him about being self-sufficient. About being a man. It's where he hoped his own son would learn a valuable lesson.

Miguel's laughs faded down the planks of the pier as he chased seagulls. The birds squawked and flapped their wings as they hopped frantically away. His red baseball cap bobbled up and down with every step as his little legs darted down the old wood.

"Miguel," yelled Robert. He waved his hands in big sweeping motions. Miguel saw him and Robert waved him over. "Be where I can see you. I'm about to set the net."

Miguel looked between his father and the birds. He abandoned the pursuit and headed back.

Robert had waited until evening to set up; that's when most fishermen packed it up for the day. There were still a few people fishing nearby, but for the most part it was quiet. He liked it this way because he could be alone with Miguel.

Miguel walked up to his father and smiled. Robert took one last drag from the cigarette, turned away from his son and exhaled a toxic cloud. He flicked the cigarette into the ocean.

"Now, I want you to watch closely," he said, pointing to his eyes then back at the rope. "I'm about to show you how to tie a proper knot and how to lower the rope, okay?"

Miguel's eyes wandered toward the

city lights. The orbs of blue and red speckled in the distance like little floating lanterns. A hand slapped the back of his head.

"Hey," said Robert. "Wake up. I'm trying to show you something."

Miguel rubbed the back of his head. He motioned with his hands, attempting to say 'sorry,' but he hadn't yet mastered sign language. He was only six years old, but even then he was learning at a rate slower than Robert would've liked.

Robert picked up a line of thin, red rope and grabbed one of the ends. His hands slowly weaved in and out as they formed a knot. He looked at Miguel. His son nodded.

Next, he looped the rope around a

wooden beam and fastened it with another knot. He gave it a tug to make sure it was secure. Robert reached into his tackle box and retrieved his knife. He pulled a fish out of his bucket and waved it at Miguel. The boy looked hesitant as he stared at the bulging eyes of the lifeless creature in front of him. Robert pressed his lips together, imitating the fish's mouth. He rolled his eyes inwards and started making kissing motions. Miguel laughed.

Robert set the fish on the floor and cut into its belly. He sliced off a large piece of flesh, exposing portions of the spine.

"This way the crabs can smell the flesh and blood," he said, waving a hand towards his nose. The boy seemed to understand and nodded.

Robert placed the fish into a mesh of thin rope, delicately placing the bait into the weaving, making sure it stayed in place. The net almost looked like a dreamcatcher with its series of metal loops and rope interlaced like webbing. He looked back to make sure his son was paying attention. Miguel's eyes were glazed as he fought off the sleep. He wasn't used to being outside this late. Robert knew his son would rather be at home reading, putting together puzzles, or even devouring his leftover Halloween candies, but he had to do this. He had to show him everything he knew.

Robert coughed so hard it scratched his throat. There wasn't much time left…months, maybe.

"Okay, now we have to make sure that

we lower the net slowly, so the fish doesn't slip out of the weaving."

He lowered the net, releasing the line little by little. After a while, the net disappeared into the black waters, and the rope lay taut on the post.

Miguel turned away to look at a couple of seagulls creeping up on the bucket of bait. They paced one webbed foot at a time, their light bodies as silent as the autumn night. He sprang at them like the monsters at the Halloween mazes. He laughed as they flew away.

Robert wiped the slime and blood off the knife and put it back in his tackle box. His fingers rifled through the box and retrieved a small lead weight and a pair of hooks.

"Okay," he said, pointing at a small rod leaning against a beam. "Get me your rod. I'm going to show you how to set it up."

Miguel waddled over to the rod in his bulky jacket, red hat, scarf, grey sweats, and small booties. His son was so layered, he reminded Robert of a mummy. He tried not to laugh to prevent himself from coughing.

The rod was cold as he took it from his son. He zipped his jacket all the way up to his neck. The sky was black now, with a wisp of clouds approaching from the ocean. Behind him, his neighbour, an old Asian man, shot up from his chair and yanked at his pole. He pulled and wrestled with his rod as if fighting an unseen phantom. After a few seconds of swift reeling, the man sat back down. The old man turned to Robert and Miguel. Robert waved a hand and smiled. The old man ignored the gesture and returned his gaze to the blackness ahead of him.

He turned to find Miguel looking intently at the beams. He traced his little fingers over old carvings of hearts and initials—lovers from years past, and mischievous children too bored to care about fishing. Robert picked up the knife and walked up to Miguel. He offered the knife.

Miguel just stared at him. Robert put the knife in his son's hand and closed his fingers on the handle.

"Just write your initials as if you were

using a pen."

He guided Miguel's hand and pressed down. The knife ground down on old, moist wood, bumping like a tattoo needle along the grooves and ridges.

When they were finished, the beam had a new chapter to its story. The letters 'MT/RT' were inscribed like runes on the beam.

They shared a smile.

"I'll just set up the rod. Go and play around," he said, shooing him off. Miguel looked confused. "Go and play; it's alright. Just be where I can see you," Robert said, pointing to his eyes again. His son smiled and waddled off.

The rod was easy to set up. It was small and flimsy and suitable for a child.

And now it probably wasn't going to be used, but that didn't matter anymore. He had taken delight in seeing him smile. He wanted to teach him as much as possible before he was gone, but if Miguel could remember one thing about his father, he was glad that it could be the ability to make him smile.

He set the rod against the beam and lit up another cigarette. He knew he shouldn't, but it didn't really matter anymore. Robert stared at the clouds again. They were bigger and had nearly blotted out the moon. Maybe there was a storm coming. He looked at his watch and wiped the moisture off. It was eight o'clock now. Where had the time gone? He remembered the doctor telling him he had maybe a year before the cancer took him away. It felt like he had received the news just a week ago.

Raising Miguel alone was difficult enough, but it was a job that was infinitely harder if you couldn't be around to do it. He had already made the funeral arrangements and had even found a distant cousin who agreed to take care of the boy. But what really upset him was the fact that there was no woman in Miguel's life. No boy should grow up without a mother.

Robert cursed Melinda under his breath for leaving them.

He looked down to find himself squeezing the knife handle. He tossed it back in the box and finished the cigarette.

Miguel was standing on a bench a few feet away, staring at the city lights again.

He was a curious one, that boy.

After a few moments, Robert thought enough time had gone by and walked to the net. He gripped the rope and pulled it up swiftly. The key was to pull as fast as possible so that the crabs wouldn't have enough time to escape the tangle of legs and netting. His forearms burned as he pulled, reaching one hand over the other. Miguel must have seen him pulling, because Robert heard his little excited grunts behind him as he pulled. The net splashed out of the ocean, but it was too dark to see.

"Hey Miggy, can you get my flashlight?" he said, closing and opening his fingers to demonstrate a flashing light. Miguel retrieved a flashlight from the tackle box and handed it to Robert.

He shined a light at the net. It was empty. The fish hadn't even been gnawed at. Robert shook his head at his son and lowered the net back into the water. Spider crabs were notoriously ugly and demonic looking, but they were delicious. Patience was always key when crab fishing. He turned and Miguel had already wandered off.

A gust of air blew in from the ocean that chilled Robert's bones. The tides swelled as they crashed louder against the pier. The smell of salty air was more potent than it had been all night.

The wind knocked Miguel's red cap off his head. Robert grabbed it before it fell into the abyss below. He walked up to

Miguel and secured it back on his head.

"I'm gonna go look and see if anyone's caught anything, okay? A storm's coming and we might have to wrap this up soon," he said, pointing at his watch and winding his finger in a circular motion. "Here," he said, pulling out a sand dollar from his pocket. "Hold on to this. It was my father's," he attempted to say in sign language. "He used to dive for clams in Mexico when he found this. He passed it on to me and now I'm giving it to you. It brings you good luck."

Miguel smiled. He examined the sand dollar in his hand. It was bleached and hard like a smooth rock. It had an imprint of a small flower in the centre. He smiled and walked off.

There were two other men fishing on the pier—his moody neighbour, and another man who appeared to be homeless, sitting quietly in the distance. None appeared to be dissuaded by the oncoming storm. Robert decided to try his hand again and walked towards the Asian man.

He paced calmly over to him as the man just stared ahead into the night. The man's pole swayed gently up and down, dancing to the currents below. Robert peered into the man's bucket. It was empty.

"Catch anything yet?" he asked as a formality, the oldest fishing ice breaker known to man.

The man turned his head in small increments, as if the very act caused pain or aggravation. His face was carved in wrinkles and marked with small liver spots. Dark circles formed under his eyes. The man had not slept in days.

"The winds are unkind tonight," he said.

"Yeah, they're really blowing in. I've yet to catch anything myself. My name's Robert, by the way," he said, extending a hand.

The man regarded the hand and extended his. He had bony fingers and long, dirty nails. Robert shook it. The hand was cold, almost as if frozen and devoid of warm, coursing blood. He did not give a name in exchange.

"I've never seen you around. This your first-time fishing here?" Robert asked.

The man nodded his head.

"Welcome. I've been fishing here all my life."

The man ignored Robert and turned to look behind him. He stared at something for a few seconds and returned his gaze to the dark sky ahead. Robert looked back and saw nothing but Miguel wandering like a lost sheep and the city lights flickering in the distance.

"What kind of bait are you using? I'm partial to mackerel or squid myself."

The old man's eyes scanned something in the dark clouds Robert couldn't make out. "I am using meat that is too old. One must always use fresh meat."

Robert looked down at the old man's tackle box. A large knife sat bloodied inside, but Robert couldn't see any sign of bait.

"Yeah, that's probably why I'm not getting it right. I bought some frozen mackerel before coming down."

"The ocean demands fresh meat, always. Something for something. It is the will of Yu-Qiang."

Robert frowned. The more he talked to the old man, the more he got a bad feeling in his stomach. He was probably senile. "Oh, who's that?"

"Yu-Qiang: the god of the ocean." The man nodded towards the fury of the waves below. "An ancient creature that lives in the deep. He is there now."

Robert looked over the support beams. Nothing but blackness and the loud crashing sounds, the only hint at a raging life below.

"Interesting. Korean legend?"

"Chinese," the old man said. "No legend. Known truth. For thousands of years we have offered our sacrifices to Yu-Qiang. He has blessed us with bounties from the sea."

"I see. Well it looks like he's on vacation tonight, huh? Maybe we'll get lucky next time," he said with a slight smile.

The old man stared ahead and said nothing.

"It was nice meeting you," Robert said, waving his hand. He stepped away and decided not to even try talking to the homeless man.

Robert felt a slight drizzle on his face

as he walked back to his spot. The moisture caught on his slight beard and made him shiver. He looked back. Miguel leaned on a beam close to the homeless man.

He waved both arms. "Hey, Miguel. Get over here. I'm gonna haul in the net."

Miguel nodded and started walking back.

The clouds were overhead now. Some of the moonlight broke through the gaps in the clouds, like a celestial body being engulfed by the dark. In a way that's how he felt about his life. It's how he pictured his lungs looking, as they struggled to take in air.

He reached inside his jacket for another smoke. The cigarette in his hand was already streaming comfort. He looked at it. The invisible bullet that had found its mark long ago. It was taking away more than his life; it was taking away his reason for life. He crushed the cigarette and dropped it at his feet.

It was time to go home.

His hands wrapped around the rope. The moisture on his fingers made the line slick and harder to pull. The rope felt heavier as he lifted.

The drizzle in the air turned to light showers as the water pelted his jacket. *Tap. Tap. Tap.* He was going to need his flashlight soon. Robert couldn't hear if Miguel was behind him but he called out anyway.

"Miguel," he shouted, raising a hand. "I need the flashlight." He opened and closed his fingers again to simulate blinking lights. The line grew heavier as he pulled; sometimes it even felt like something pulled back. Something angry.

He heard the net emerge from the ocean, as water dripped in torrents underneath. It was too dark to see but he felt the net swaying side to side. Whatever it was, it was big.

"Miguel?" Robert looked back. Miguel wasn't visible. The light showers turned to heavy rain. Visibility was reduced as the falling streaks of water filled the air. The homeless man in the distance sat motionless as he watched his pole swaying violently.

He went back to pulling. Hand after hand, he heaved, trying not to lose his grip.

He looked back again. The Chinese man reeled in a large mojarra fish. It gasped for breath on the floor as the water reaching its mouth filled its lungs with false hope.

Robert called out again, the panic now filling his voice. "Miguel!" He coughed. Blood spewed onto his hands. He ignored the cold in his bones and the fire in his lungs and pulled. The net was at eye level and he saw movement. A lot of movement. He swung the net over the beams, and it landed on the planks.

A swarm of spider crabs spilled over the rims of the net. Their long, angled legs stabbed indiscriminately in every direction.

Down the pier, the old Chinese man carried a pail full of fish as water collected and spilled from the sides. He faded into the damp night.

He had to look for Miguel. He called out again. "Miguel?"

Robert peered over the edges. There was no sign of the boy. He tried to listen for his grunts. Nothing.

The homeless man. Robert ran towards the man, careful not to slip on the wet floor.

"Excuse me? Excuse me, sir? Have you seen a little boy?"

The man made no gesture.

Maybe he didn't hear.

Robert put a hand to his shoulder and shook gently.

Nothing.

Robert shook harder. The man's head rolled back—his mouth open to the falling rains. A large chunk of flesh was missing from his throat. Blood seeped down his neck, mixing with the rainwater. Robert took a step back and slipped on the slick planks. His head slammed on the wood and he coughed up more blood. He pushed himself up. The spider crabs were crawling over the floor like angered monsters.

In the distance, something caught his eye.

He hurried towards the net. He picked up his flashlight and shone the light on the crabs. Mandibles tore into minuscule bits of flesh. He picked up the crabs and tossed them aside. There were so many. His hands scraped and nicked against the sharp shells. He didn't care. He had to know.

And it was there.

His lungs seized. His breaths became

short and painful.

He fell to his knees amidst a mass of clambering legs. A bounty from the sea. *Something for something*, the old man had said. *Fresh meat*.

Robert Tapia picked up the red cap and stared at the small, unidentifiable head in front of him.

The dark waters swayed and crashed against the pier as the tempest pressed ahead.

He lay down next to his boy.

Thorny legs overtook his body as his howls faded into the cold, autumn night.

First published in *Online*, Crystal Lake Publishing, October 2016

NEW WORLD

By R.J. Meldrum

John and Amanda stared out the front window of their house, desperately looking for some sign, some update from the outside. For the last few days, the city streets had been almost completely empty, just an occasional car whizzed past. There were no pedestrians. The city looked deserted.

The lockdown had been in place for four months. Stay at home, no non-essential travel. They had stocked up and obeyed. During the first couple of weeks the lockdown had been almost fun, a chance to work from home, to eat and drink too much. After the first month it got a little tense, being stuck indoors all day, only allowed out for essential travel. They couldn't visit their friends or their families and that hit them hard, but they still obeyed. The constant fear of infection was enough for them to obey.

The news was rarely good. Cases were increasing, hospitals were overloaded. The dead were left in the street, covered by blankets. Stores were running short of the most basic items. Fear was etched on the faces of the news anchors, as they reported the daily mortality count and lack of an effective treatment.

As the weeks passed, the shortages became extreme; there were riots, looters on the streets. They no longer wanted to leave their home, despite running short of food. They heard shooting in the distance.

And now, they were completely isolated. The internet had been down for five days; the power had failed yesterday. No cellphone reception. From what they could see from their window, they were alone.

"Should we leave?"

"Where? We don't have a car."

"I don't know."

There was a scratching at the front door.

"See, someone is outside. Maybe it's the police," said John.

He walked to the front door.

"Darling, don't open the door!" shouted Amanda.

It was too late. He'd already opened the door a crack by the time she shouted her warning. The city rats, uncontrolled and starving after weeks of lockdown, pushed through and swarmed over them.

THE RAVEN'S REVENGE

By Raven Corinn Carluk

Fall nights came too damn early. Buster huddled deeper into his jacket, cursing the long and lonely dirt road. Darkness always fell too damn suddenly, dropping the temperature too damn much, making his walks home too damn miserable.

Caw.

His head snapped up, a sharp frown creasing his forehead. It was after dark, and all the pesky crows should be asleep. Yet this one sounded close by, in a tree to the left. Buster increased his pace, wanting to get past the row of trees as fast as possible. Where there was one crow, there were others.

A long croak sounded from high above, almost as if it were taunting him. "Get outta here, hellbeast!" he shouted at the top of his lungs. Were it daylight, he'd have chucked a rock, like normal. "Filthy things don't belong here."

Caw.

The sound chilled him, scared him so much that it made him angry. Logically, Buster knew they were only birds. But it wasn't logic that was in control. Irrational loathing of their beady eyes and sooty feathers made him lash out.

His kill count was at thirty-five for the month.

Not that killing them made much of a difference. There were always more crows, like they replenished their numbers from some demon gate. Always watching, always making noise, always wanting his soul.

Caw. Caw. Caw.

Three of them, in different trees, loud and disconcerting. Buster's heart raced.

Why were they up this late? Could they see him in the dark? He wanted to be home and behind locked doors like nothing else.

As he scurried down the road, rustling and muttering came from the trees. Far more than three birds. Buster would have sworn there were a thousand nasty crows glaring at him. "Just fuck off!" Too bad he didn't have his .22 pistol with him. *Then* those pests would leave him alone.

With the sound of a hell chorus, the crows took flight. Cawing, flapping, rustling, they were coming for him, finally ready to claim his soul. Buster shrieked and fled, not caring if anyone thought him a coward. Didn't matter what grown men were and weren't supposed to do.

His headlong race didn't last long. A

hole caught his foot, sent him crashing to the ground. Buster's head struck a rock, and stars danced before his eyes.

The crows cawed madly, as if cackling over his fall.

Fighting through his dizziness, Buster got to his feet. Knowing he would be attacked at any moment, he stumbled forward, determined to make it home. He wasn't going to let the monster flock circling overhead have a chance to get him. Weakly, he pulled his jacket over his head, seeking even a feeble defence.

Caw.

A vicious bird dove at him, clawing at his exposed skin, wings battering his covered flesh.

Buster swore and dodged to the side.

He lost his balance, stumbled off the dirt road and to the edge of a culvert. His heart lodged in his throat as he tried not to fall.

Another bird swooped down at him, and Buster fell. The ditch was deep, full of rocks, and he landed with a sharp crack of his neck. Sobbing and paralyzed, he could only watch as the demon birds descended for their meal. "Now I see...a murder of crows."

BEYOND THE JUNIPER GROVE

By Rich Rurshell

Don't stray beyond the grove of juniper trees.

Adahy's words played on my mind as I stepped between the gnarled trunks of the

225

first two junipers. There were rumours about this part of the forest. Everybody avoided it. The logging crews, the local hunters, even the native Americans. But my guess is, that's why those teenagers headed out here in the first place. To make a video for their YouTube channels or something. There were three boys and two girls, and they had been missing for a week. Regardless of their reasons, I was here to find them. Alone.

I hadn't set out alone. There had been a number of us when the search party first entered the forest. Several hunters, some of the teenagers' family members, other good folk from the local area. And Adahy, a native American of about my age.

He was certainly useful in getting us

on the right track, but all of his talk about what lies in the midst of the forest was the main contributing factor to my being alone. Wendigos, living trees, fearsome beasts, and of course, the spirit of the forest. That's what troubled him most. I thought it was all folklore and legends from his people's history, not to be taken at face value, but the others took it all seriously. Alongside local rumors, and the disappearance of the five teenagers, Adahy's tales had them all turning back as the sun began to set. Adahy went with them to ensure they found their way home safely.

As the milky white light of the setting sun shone through the canopy of the forest, I pressed on through the twisted trunks of the ancient junipers.

Before long, I came upon the corpse of a white stag. A hart. Its body riddled with bullet holes, dark red blood staining its pale fur. Since the hunters don't dare stray into the depths of the forest, I could only assume those kids had come armed. And were trigger-happy too. The creature's tongue hung from its mouth, thick with blood, and its eye stared unseeing skyward. Although it was getting dark, I felt I was getting close. I took out my flashlight from my pack and ventured further into the forest.

***

At first, I heard the occasional sound of twigs snapping behind the rows of trees on either side of me. Shining my flashlight into the darkness beyond, I tried to see what was causing the noises, but found nothing. Then came the whispers. Barely audible. Loud enough to know they were there, but not enough to hear what they were saying. The snapping became louder, more frequent. I spun around, pointing the beam of light towards the source of the sounds.

Nothing.

"Hello?"

I got no reply. Just more whispers and even louder snapping, like branches being broken. I backed away and something touched my shoulder. I turned and found myself snagged on a branch. I pulled away, tearing my shirt, only to become caught on another. I lashed out with the flashlight and broke free. A low moan came from the trees around me.

I shuddered. Something moved beyond the twisted tree trunks in my light beam, disappearing into the darkness behind the trees. I turned to run, but tripped and fell to the ground. My hand fell into something wet. It came up covered in blood. Beneath me, in the torchlight, I found a corpse. A human corpse. Or at least what was left.

Josh Warwick. I could only identify him from a tattoo on his upper arm that was shown on the missing person report. His head was gone, his torso ripped open. Empty. As I scrambled to my feet in a panic, a monstrous bellow came from deeper in the forest.

My heart racing, I fled away from whatever made that ungodly sound.

Branches tore at my face and clothes as I ran, my flashlight torn from my hands. Deafening snapping sounds came from all sides, following me as I ran blindly through the forest, my hands held out in front of me to avoid running into trees. An eerie green light emanated from deep within the trees in front of me, so I ran towards it, disoriented, the strange light giving me my only bearings.

The cacophony of humming, whispering, and breaking wood surrounded me as I raced towards the light. I ran into a clearing.

Then there was silence.

Before me, in the centre of the clearing, stood a huge oak tree. Wooden torches sat within its branches, burning with green fire.

Then I noticed her. And the horror that surrounded her.

Crouching beneath the lower branches of the oak, with her back to me, was a woman. She was completely naked, nursing a large boar which lay taking shallow breaths, its coarse fur bloodstained. Around them were the mutilated remains of the other missing teenagers. It was impossible to tell who was who, their bodies torn to pieces and scattered around the base of the mighty oak.

The woman slowly got to her feet and turned to face me. Her pale skin shimmered green in the torchlight as she approached, her footfalls silent. Long black hair hung around her shoulders and down her back. She stared right into me with eyes as black as night.

All manner of feelings filled my mind. My very soul. I feared her, loved her, wanted her. My heart raced, and I felt panic building inside me, and yet a pulsing erection formed in my trousers. I wanted to run, and never return, yet part of me wanted to stay. Stay with her in the forest, forever. Worship her, ravish her, bend to her every will. I shivered and began to cry.

She smiled. The smile promised love, pleasure, peace, comfort, and yet I understood hatred, danger, and disgust from her. She was perfect. Everything I wanted. Everything I feared. She pulled my every emotion from within me with her very presence. Then she was standing right before me.

She placed her hand on my chest, over my heart. I shook with terror, a scream building up in my throat. Then she leant forward and kissed me.

I screamed, and a powerful orgasm exploded in my loins.

I lost consciousness…

***

I am the spirit of the forest. Your kind are not welcome here. You are not welcome here. Those who come here and disrespect my domain, shall be destroyed. Those who cause pain and destruction in my forest have felt my wrath. Pain beyond your wildest fears. Terror beyond your comprehension. I am all-knowing, understand everything. I am nature, and I have looked into your heart. You have come for those who came before you, but there is nothing remaining of them for you. Your intentions are good, but your presence here will no longer be tolerated. Leave this forest with your life, and never return.

I have spoken...

***

I woke up shivering in complete darkness, my body aching and sore all over.

"Begone," she whispered.

I jumped to my feet. Blindly stepping forwards, I stumbled into a wall of warmth and wet fur.

An almighty roar shook the forest.

Whatever I'd heard bellow earlier was

235

right there, towering over me. I turned and fled in terror, into the trees, hoping to find my way back to civilization, and out of the forest beyond the juniper grove.

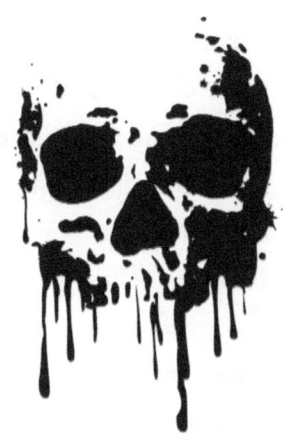

THE DEMON CAT

By Destiny Eve Pifer

Outside, the wind and rain pounded against the old, weathered porch. Chains rattled as the wind grew strong. Leila awoke from her nap to find that darkness had filled the once bright sky. Though the fire was still roaring, she couldn't help but find the air quite chill. Suddenly she heard a strange noise coming from the patio door. She quietly rose and tried switching on the light, only to find that the electricity had gone out. Grabbing a flashlight from her desk, she began walking down the dark hallway. Under her breath, she silently cursed her husband, Peter, for being out of town on business. With her kids away in college, she was all alone.

As she made her way into the dining room, she heard a scratching at the door. She quietly walked over and opened the curtains to find a small black cat looking up at her. Its yellow eyes appeared to be glowing. As it started to mew, she couldn't help but feel compelled to let it in. After all, it was cold outside, and the poor thing was shivering. She opened the door and let him in. Tonight, she would have a new companion. However, she couldn't be more wrong. That night as the storm raged on, her faith would be tested by a small furry stranger. She laid down a bowl of milk only to find that the cat wasn't one bit interested. Instead, it appeared to be more interested in exploring the house.

She found the cat looking up at her husband's birds that he kept caged and in his office. As she reached out to pet the cat, it jumped away and scurried into the darkness. She tried following the cat, but lost sight of him. Not thinking much of her new furry friend, she went back to sit in front of the fireplace. She picked up a book, but suddenly felt her eyes too heavy to read. She had no sooner dozed off when she heard a crash from the other room. Jumping up, she rushed into the office and found the cage lying on the ground and opened. One of the birds was injured while the other was missing. She knelt down and shined the light on the cage and was about to rescue the bird when her hand touched something slimy. She looked down at her hand and found it covered with blood. She looked up just in time to see the cat pouncing on top of the cage. In his mouth he held the broken and bloody body of the one bird, and using his paw, he knocked something down into the cage.

She looked down in horror at the bird's head which had been torn from its body.

She angrily swatted at the cat, only for it to hiss and claw at her hand. With deep wounds in her hand, she stumbled to her feet and fled into the bedroom. She made sure the door was locked, then headed to the sink. As she began cleaning the wounds, she could hear something clawing at the door. She looked down and saw tiny paws reaching under the door. She could feel her heart pounding against her chest and her hands were now shaking. It was two in the morning and she was trapped in the bathroom hiding from a deranged cat. She opened the cabinets and pulled out her husband's shaving razor, which had been passed down to him. By then the scratching had stopped. She leaned down and looked out the keyhole but didn't see any movement. As she silently opened the door, her body began to shake.

Never had she been more terrified than she was now. She knew that the only way to make it to the front door was to walk down the dark hallway. Once she made it outside, then she could run for help, but right now the game was on. Somewhere in the darkness the cat was lurking and waiting. Why it had chosen to terrorise her, she had no idea. She had just made it to the dining room when the cat leaped from the top of the fridge and onto her head. She stumbled and fell backwards as it began clawing at her face. She shoved it away only for it to come back. This time she swung the razor blade and got it in the paw. However, it only made the cat more furious. It sank its teeth into her hand and wouldn't let go until she dropped the razor blade. She slammed her hand against the wall hoping it would let go, but it only sank its fangs deeper into her flesh.

She cried out in pain as she began crawling towards the knife drawer. She pulled the drawer out and knives soon fell to the floor, making a clanging noise that echoed through the darkness. She was about to reach for a knife when the cat lunged forward and sank claws into the back of her neck. She began rolling on the floor until the cat finally let go. She then watched as it scurried off into the darkness. Grabbing a large butcher knife, she headed out into the hallway only to be met with a loud noise. Without another thought, she waved the knife through the air and heard someone moan then fall to the floor. As the lights came back on, she was horrified to find that it was her husband she had stabbed. Letting out a scream, she dropped the knife, as the cat sat high up on the bookshelves looking down at her. With its mission accomplished, it leaped down and hurried out into the darkness.

AN ETERNITY TOGETHER

By Stephen Herczeg

Sammi sipped from her drink and glanced at Victor. She wanted to play this right. He was the most gorgeous man she had ever dated in her short life. His long raven black hair hung down and framed his Adonis like face. His clear, porcelain like skin only broken up by the dark, thin eyebrows and pencil moustache.

They had met only a month before, but Sammi was already head over heels in love with him. She loved talking to him through the long, cold nights. She loved the stories he told of his life. He had fitted so many adventures into his time on the planet, from joyous revelry through to tales of terror that would frighten even the sternest of hearts. He was never at a loss for words, or new tales to tell.

She had made her decision. She knew it was too soon. She knew that her few friends would say she was nuts, but she had made up her mind. She wanted to stay with

Victor for the rest of eternity.

Sammi took another sip and put her glass down. She reached out and placed her hand on top of Victor's.

Looking into his eyes, she said, "I've made up my mind."

"And?"

"I want to be with you. Forever."

He smiled.

"It is a big decision. Life with me is not easy all the time."

She nodded.

"I know there will be those that won't understand."

"Your family?"

Sammi's face screwed up.

"I don't care what they think. They think I'm a burden. They've never loved me, not like you. My thoughts are the same. I'd be happy to be rid of the lot of them. For years I've wished them dead."

"Your friends?"

"I don't have that many close friends. Not like you. They certainly have never been close unlike your family. They'll miss me for a while, but my memory will fade. Probably sooner than even I could believe."

Victor smiled again and took a sip of his own drink.

"It is rare that someone offers themselves to me so willingly. Many of my family were the opposite, but over time they came to accept their fate."

He stared into Sammi's eyes. She felt his gaze piercing deep into her mind, into her soul. He seemed to be reading her most hidden thoughts. Making sure that she knew what she wanted and what was involved.

After a moment he smiled again and nodded.

"Yes. You are ready."

He moved a lock of hair away from her neck.

"Now, when I make someone like me, it can hurt."

"I'm prepared for it."

She braced herself.

Victor smiled and opened his mouth. His fangs slid out from the gum sheaths. He thrust his head forward and sank them deep into Sammi's neck.

She screamed in spite of herself.

BLACK HARE PRESS

TAKEN

By Ximena Escobar

I saw her silhouette sever from the shadows, the hem of her dress sweeping the earth like serpents exuding at her every step, as she entered the radiance of the bonfire and forced me to bear her form.

Orange flared in her nearing pupils, widening, swallowing something—my whole life, perhaps. I saw myself ablaze in her eyes, her reptilian tongue slithering out of her purple lips, and I felt the burning heat consume me from within, that with every lick she soothed me, as her long black hair enveloped me like a protecting palm, and I became a flame.

ABOUT THE PUBLISHER

BLACK HARE PRESS is a small, independent publisher based in Melbourne, Australia.

Founded in 2018, our aim has always been to champion emerging authors from all around the globe and offer opportunities for them to participate in speculative fiction and horror short story anthologies.

Connect

Website: *www.blackharepress.com*

Twitter: *@BlackHarePress*

BLACK HARE PRESS

www.ingramcontent.com/pod-product-compliance
Lightning Source LLC
Chambersburg PA
CBHW032002130726
47903CB00012B/677